ILLUSTRATED NOVELS:
A New Art Form for a New Age

They say a picture's worth a thousand words...and they're right.
As anyone who's seen a movie and then read the book it's based on
can tell you, every media has its own strengths, things it can do better
than any other form. And that's what illustrated novels bring:
the strengths of two different media—strong, elegant, cinematic prose
and detailed illustrations that speak volumes to the reader.

The power of prose
combined with the beauty
of rich illustrations.

TAD WILLIAMS

MIRROR WORLD

AN ILLUSTRATED NOVEL

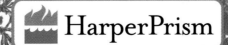

HarperPrism

A Division of HarperCollins*Publishers*
10 East 53rd Street, New York, NY 10022

Designed by Michael Chatham

*With sincere appreciation to Robert Gottlieb and Matt Bieler
of William Morris Agency, and to Frank Curtis, Esq.,
for all their work on our behalf.*

*HarperPrism books may be purchased for educational, business, or sales
promotional use. For information, please write:
Special Markets Department, HarperCollinsPublishers,
10 East 53rd Street, New York, NY 10022-5299.*

ISBN: 0-06-105545-X

Printed in the United States of America

First Printing: June 1998

*Visit HarperPrism on the World Wide Web at
http://www.harperprism.com*

98 99 00 01 ❖/RRD 10 9 8 7 6 5 4 3 2

TAD WILLIAMS'
MIRROR WORLD

Table of Contents

Introduction

In June of 1999, a strange phenomenon appeared in the world's major cities. Giant mirrors split the cities in half. Bisecting buildings, cutting through roads, parks, and pathways, the Mirrors were beautiful and completely inexplicable. People were fascinated by them. But the Mirrors were much more than the curiosities they seemed. People discovered they could step through those Mirrors into another world.

Soon, adventurous souls everywhere were taking the trip. In the beginning, the Mirrored surfaces were two-way, letting citizens of our world travel through them to this strange new world and then return. Thousands did so. Then the Mirrors in that new world vanished. The curious sightseers were stranded forever on the planet they came to call Mirrorworld.

A trip through Earth's Mirrors now became a one-way journey. What started out as a curious odyssey became a permanent exile.

Even after this was common knowledge, people still crossed the Mirrors—some to find loved ones stranded on the other side, some to challenge new frontiers, some to fight back against the horrors coming through the Mirrors and threatening all of society.

For, back on Earth, the Mirrors finally revealed their purpose. Giant predatory creatures, obviously insectoid in nature, poured through the Mirrors in swarms, killing or carrying off everything living in their path. The Bugs, as they were called, were a deadly plague. And they just kept coming.

It became clear that the answer to the problem was to seek out the home of the Bugs and destroy it. The Mirrors could appear anywhere without warning, so there was no way to predict an attack or defend against the Bugs unless the people of Earth attacked the problem at the source. The source was somewhere on the other side of those Mirrors. Because the problem was worldwide, the United Nations tackled it.

The U.N. had learned something crucial from those who had crossed the Mirrors and returned. Nothing inorganic survived the trip. Everything that wasn't organic—plastic, metal, stone, or whatever—vanished on the far side of that barrier. From fillings to false teeth, from weapons to polyester clothing, it was gone when the bearer crossed the Mirrors.

Conventional modern weapons, therefore, were completely useless as the world met this threat. The U.N. took sixty volunteers and augmented them physically—transplants, hormonal stimulation, mental synapse rerouting—until they were faster, smarter, or stronger than humanly possible. The augmentation process had its drawbacks. It was painful and dangerous—only thirty-seven of the first sixty volunteers survived it.

The augmentation process couldn't guarantee the loyalty, the sanity, or the determination of the people who underwent the transformation. But these soldiers, thinkers, and athletes were the best the world could offer to stop the plague. The biotroopers, as they were called, went through the Mirrors to perform their mission.

When they got there, there made an amazing discovery. The world on the other side of the Mirrors had alien animals and plants, many quite dangerous, but no higher life-forms, and no giant Bugs. The menace they'd come to fight was nowhere in sight. The biotroopers could only conclude that somewhere on this world, far away from where they'd landed, were other Mirrors, serving as a conduit to still other worlds.

The discovery took the heart out of most of the biotroopers. When they arrived in Mirrorworld, the situation on the other side of the glass was so appalling that many of the biotroopers decided they had more than enough to do to improve the terrible conditions that the new settlers were coping with.

The few biotroopers who went on to pursue the Bugs had their own reasons for doing so—some altruistic, some more selfish. The rest of the troopers remained in the new cities they founded or discovered, sometimes to help the inhabitants, sometimes to rule them absolutely.

In the anarchy of those early days, the biotroopers carved out territories and protectorates, some benign, some evil beyond words. Once the initial lines in the sand were drawn, each city developed its own agenda. Some looked around for new worlds to conquer, others sought to form alliances for mutual protection. The political situation was uncertain, and it was clear even to the idealists that only the strongest would survive. It was a frontier life on an alien world— with all of the opportunities and hazards that entailed.

It is now years after humans first crossed through to Mirrorworld. Established territories include the city-states Shades and Looking Glass, benign cities where many of the biotroopers make their homes.

Between these two cities is the downtrodden territory of Darklea. There, secure in a fortress called The Hospital, an evil biotrooper known only as "Father" schemes to take over the lands surrounding him.

But the vast majority of Mirrorworld is uncharted land, a wilderness waiting to be discovered. Out on the fringes of Mirrorworld, many thousands of people struggle to survive, to build a life on an alien planet, to begin again in a place that nothing could prepare them for.

Some of their stories are collected here, in this volume.

So turn the page to begin a voyage to a whole new world...Mirrorworld.

MIRROR ~IN~ TIME

written by
Mark Kreighbaum

illustrated by
Ron Mahoney

Threnodies

Dancer labored up the slope of the hill. He used his walking stick to clear the chest-high black and yellow grass from his path. Sap from the grass smeared his clothes, hands, and face. It smelled like rancid butter. He still wasn't used to it, even after days of traveling through the stuff.

Birdsong filled the air, but no bird ever heard on Earth had sung so magnificently. The calls reminded him of wind-chimes and flutes. He half-closed his eyes. The muscles in his legs strained as he struggled forward. Shadows lengthened before him and a breeze that heralded the coming dusk chilled his sweat. Just a little further, he told himself, the old mantra that had carried him through every marathon he'd ever run back on Earth. Then he'd been competing against himself, against the clock. Now his life and everything he'd ever hoped for hung in the balance.

He paused occasionally to look around him with a wary gaze. He didn't think Joah and Kat had passed this way, but he'd rather be overcautious than caught in one of Joah's clever little traps.

The sun had nearly set when he finally reached the peak. The sky had a quiet amber glow shot through with streaks of pale red and gold. He missed the purple and crimson glory of sunsets on Earth. He missed a lot of things from home.

Dancer fought through a last dense patch of the grass to a clearing. There, burnished by the fading sun, he saw the thing that had been calling to his mind for many days and miles, that was still calling to him even now, flaming in his thoughts like a beacon. He'd expected something immense. But the source of the signal was only an arch of old green stone, not the powerful psionic machine he'd expected, nor the wise race of telepaths he'd secretly hoped for. Just a collection of stones shaped like the tori of a Shinto shrine, two pillars of green marble supporting a curve of lighter jade with what looked like a mortise and tenon joint, like the trilithons of Stonehenge. Several of the shrines were spaced around the grassy clearing, emphasizing the resemblance to the mysterious artifact on the Salisbury plain.

A surprisingly strong wave of disappointment made him stagger. He had been so sure that he would find help here. He leaned on his walking stick, a solid staff of polished wood that resembled mahogany.

"Well, ain't that bright?" he murmured, repeating one of his father's favorite expressions. His voice sounded shaky and querulous in his ears. It made him feel nervous. He'd been talking to himself a lot lately. "Just as long as nobody's answering," he said. But the weak joke didn't ease his discomfort. He was nearing a mental precipice that he hoped and prayed he wouldn't go over.

Dancer sighed, then walked to one of the stone structures. Closer study made him think even more of Stonehenge. The rock was smooth, carefully dressed. He knew a fair bit about masonry, thanks to his grandfather, and his practiced eyes picked out the niches where wedges would have been struck and ropes would have been set for hauling. The stones in the circle were celadon in hue, with a generous vein of deeper green. Irregular chips of a jade-like stone were inset along the lintel. He stared at the shapes, squinting into the slanting rays of the sunset. Hard to tell, but it looked like the jade formed some kind of design, some kind of message. So, maybe this place *was* a shrine. His quick examination of the other stones turned up nothing new.

Whatever its purpose, the dance of stones sang out to his mind as if its pillars were strings in a storm-tossed aeloian harp. Hesitantly, he touched a palm to one of the uprights, but nothing registered. It was only cold stone. But in his mind, the artifact continued to call, though more softly with the dying of the light. It was only when the sun vanished over the horizon that the call was silenced, its absence a ringing void in Dancer's mind.

"Powered by the sun, maybe?" he murmured.

"Sure, why not?" said a familiar voice. "Maybe it's the Mirrorworld version of a solar-powered telephone, eh?"

Dancer turned around. A man with a shaved head and eyes that glowed golden in the dark grinned at him. He wore layers of animal skins for clothes and, like Dancer, carried a walking stick. It didn't surprise Dancer that he could see the man clearly in a darkness penetrated only by the light of the distant stars. It frightened him, though, that he couldn't tell if this image was a psychic sending, or one of the increasingly vivid visions that plagued him. Dancer judged Joah's mood and decided that this time his old friend wouldn't try to kill him.

"Hello, Joah," said Dancer. "I should have known you'd have heard the call, too."

Joah smiled and leaned on his walking stick. "Unlike you, I detoured around it. Curiosity is going to be the death of you, my friend."

"That detour is going to cost you," Dancer replied. "How far ahead of me are you now? A week? Four days? You've been slowing down."

"You should have stayed in Looking Glass, Dancer." Joah's image looked mildly threatening.

"Yeah, right." Dancer sat down with his back against one of the stone pillars. It felt wonderful to stretch out his legs and massage his strained muscles. "You left a little mess back there, you and Kat."

Joah shrugged and seated himself on some invisible log or rock.

"It didn't have to go that way. How were we to know that Father booby-trapped the books we gave to the library? We didn't mean for anyone to get hurt. We were just trying to slow you down."

"Yeah. Sure," Dancer said. He could tell Joah wasn't telling the truth—or at least not all of the truth.

It seemed Joah didn't like Dancer's tone. Dancer could tell that from the hunch of Joah's shoulders and the narrowing of his eyes.

"This is war, Daniel. Rain and Blue and all those other pathetic *pioneers*," Joah's voice twisted on the word, "think they're carving a society out of the wilderness. They're fools and traitors. You could say we executed a few deserters."

Dancer's face tightened. But he knew better than to show his anger to Joah's projection. His former colleague would just cut off contact. Joah couldn't abide emotional displays—that was ironic, because the man himself was so deeply passionate about so many things.

"And you're a loyal trooper, I suppose?" Dancer asked, evenly.

"The Bugs'll wipe out this world's pitiful mockeries of cities in a day when they come back. And believe me, Daniel, the Bugs are coming back. I've seen them, descending from the sky like the fall of a thousand stars." Joah's golden eyes burned in the darkness like candles.

"Where are you going, Joah? Tell me where you're going," Dancer whispered. Sometimes, when Joah was like this, he would speak at length, tell Dancer anything.

This time, however, Joah looked away and his expression changed, softened into serenity, clarity. He was talking to Kat, Dancer knew. Dancer felt an ache like an ancient hunger. Maxwell Blue, an old friend, was one of the few people in this universe that understood what Dancer was up to—why he *had* to follow Joah and Kat. Alone among all the people in the city of Looking Glass, Maxwell had understood why Dancer had to move on after he'd helped them fight off Father's latest attack. Maxwell knew all about the Triptych Project. He understood that Dancer could no more stop running after Kat and Joah then he could cease breathing. Blue knew all about unrequited love. And, like Dancer, he knew that Kat and Dancer working in tandem were Mirrorworld's only hope of luring Joah back over the borderline between sanity and madness. A crazed Joah wasn't just dangerous to those in his immediate vicinity. He was dangerous to them all. As Dancer had left Looking Glass, Blue had waved his friend off with a smile. That had been a long time ago. In the months since then, Dancer had learned patience. He waited.

Joah turned back to Dancer.

"You know where we're going, Daniel," the image said, softly. Joah's features split into a grin just a hair short of madness. Dancer tensed. Would he attack now? "We're on our way to Mere to see the Wizard."

Dancer shook his head, but didn't let down his guard. Joah's mental attacks could be so quick. "Mere's a myth, Joah. A kind of Mirrorworld version of El Dorado. You're chasing a fairy tale."

"Oh, it's real, my friend."

"Come on, Joah. Don't waste your life looking for a city that doesn't exist. Come back with me to Looking Glass, you and Kat. We'll . . . we'll be together."

Joah studied Dancer with an expression of infinite compassion. For this brief moment, the old Joah Cray was looking out of those strange glowing golden eyes, once again—for a single instant—the dear friend who understood so much of his heart. Too much.

"You could join us," said Joah. "We could all be a team again.

Kat and I miss you. We're going to need you when we find the Bugs."

Dancer was tempted, so tempted. But he remembered the twisted bodies and flaming wreckage Joah had left behind in Looking Glass, all because he didn't care about the consequences of his obsession with the Bugs. Joah's mind had broken. Perhaps only Kat kept him sane at this point. If he joined them, how long would it be before—somewhere out there in the trackless wilderness—Joah killed them all in some fit of madness, while they hunted for an illusion?

Just two days ago, Joah had done his best to fry Dancer's mind in a psychic attack. Dancer hadn't ruled out the possibility that all the weird visions and hallucinations he'd been suffering from lately were Joah's doing. Joah Cray was capable of anything now.

"No, Joah," Dancer replied sadly. "You know that could never work, not now. You're…you're not well."

"Then go back to Looking Glass, Dancer. Kat and I don't need you. The deserters there can use men who've forgotten their purpose."

"Let me talk to Kat. I need—"

But Joah vanished, leaving Dancer alone in deep darkness, shivering. For awhile, Dancer simply sat with his back against the stone and his eyes closed. Questions buzzed in his head like angry wasps. What had happened to Joah? How had his closest friend lost his mental balance? Was it a result of the Triptych Project that had made the three of them into telepaths? Or was there something more fundamentally broken in Joah? Why had he kidnapped Kat and taken her through the Mirror? What could he possibly hope to accomplish here in the middle of nowhere?

Not even Maxwell Blue believed that the Bugs remained on Mirrorworld. Blue had been here for a decade.

But these questions paled before the most important ones. *Why does Kat stay with him?* Dancer raged. *Why is she running from me? Why won't she talk to me?* Kat could have broken away from Joah in Looking Glass, if she'd wanted to, but she chose to stay with him. Chose to help Joah—never mind the devastation that Joah left everywhere in his path.

Dancer couldn't believe that Kat didn't care about the dead bodies Joah left strewn behind them. At least one witness to Father's attack and its aftermath had said Kat had been the one who'd warned the people in the library about the bomb.

Dancer clung to that thought, to his belief that Kat still retained her sanity, and prayed that he wasn't deluding himself. He would never succeed in stopping Joah without Kat's help.

He shook his head and closed his eyes more tightly. He could feel the

hot sting of tears again. *Why are you running away from me, Kat?* But no matter how hard Dancer tried to reach her, Kat's mind was closed to him. From the beginning, Dancer's telepathy had always worked best with Joah, though if Kat and Dancer were physically close together, Dancer could touch her thoughts, too. The memory of that bond which, for Dancer, satisfied a need that ran deeper than hunger, tormented him.

Exhausted, Dancer ate a bit of jerky, drank some water—brackish from the animal skin he carried it in—and unrolled his tattered down and silk sleeping bag by the side of one of the massive stone pillars. He shouldn't go to sleep here. It was an unprotected, indefensible position. But he didn't have the energy or heart to bother scouting the perimeter, setting up warning trip wires and snares. If he was killed while he slept, so be it. A tiny part of him even welcomed the prospect. He settled into his bedroll, pillowed his head against his backpack, and let the night take him.

Dancer fell into a deep sleep. Soon, he dreamed.

❧ ❦

In the dream, Dancer was a ten-year-old child tagging along behind his two older brothers on a hike in Colorado. He had the feeling that Jack and Brian didn't know he was there and that they would be angry if they found out, so he crept along in their wake as quietly as he could. Mom and Dad were somewhere else, not ahead, not behind. They were all climbing a trail. It was Dancer's first time on a real hike. Jack and Brian were talking to each other, a murmur like water flowing, and Dancer couldn't distinguish the words, but he knew somehow that they were talking about Mom, that they were worried.

His brothers wore their weathered hiking packs, massive aluminum frames jammed with all sorts of camping gear. Those packs were as familiar to Dancer as his brothers' faces. He realized suddenly that he, too, was wearing his pack, the stripped-down version that his father had put together for him. The pack felt light as air, and this made Dancer feel unexpectedly guilty, almost ashamed.

The scene shifted abruptly and he was at a picnic with dozens of people, family and friends. Everyone was there: Dad and Mom, Grampa, the cousins, kids from school. Dancer was lying on his back staring at the sky. This was a dream of a memory, but not Dancer's. But there was a connection between the two, if he could only think of it.

The deep blue sky was peppered with dots of blackness, as if a thousand tiny black clouds were gathering high up. Then the dots became larger and larger until their true nature became clear: the Bugs! The sky was filled with Bugs.

Dancer's dream self leapt up as the Bugs swooped down and crushed and killed all of the people at the picnic, everyone he knew and loved. Screams—and worse—filled the air. He heard them dying all around him.

He ran.

He ran as fast as he could, but the world spun still faster beneath his feet. Behind him came the whirr of wings, whispering, whispering. He could almost understand the words. He would spend the rest of his life trying to understand, but also constructing a black pearl of rage around this tragedy.

He ran.

◄8 8►

The artifact woke Dancer with a whisper, a tickle of sound on the verge of morning. False dawn, the color of tarnished brass, tinged the clearing. Dancer tried to hold the dream a bit longer, but it faded away, leaving no memories, only an ache of vague guilt and fear. Something about his mother, he guessed.

Dancer yawned, sat up, and spent a few moments scratching his bug bites. One thing Mirrorworld had in common with Earth was an abundance of blood-sucking insects. Finally he stood up and stretched—felt the pull and ache of muscles he'd abused during yesterday's long climb. He ran a hand over his face.

Dancer looked around idly at the artifact and was shocked to see an

alien creature sitting cross-legged beneath the arch across from him.

Slender and covered with a fine reddish colored hair, the alien stared at him from eyes slitted behind heavy epicanthic folds. The creature's skull was triangular, ridged, and bony, and its joints were oddly articulated, as if the flesh concealed multiple elbows and knees. It wore an embroidered vest with drawstring pockets and a kilt dyed gray and yellow, belted with a silver cord. The alien wore no jewelry, except for a slender bracelet of silver metal on one forearm. It watched him calmly, disinterestedly.

Clearly, this was a civilized creature, one who probably had encountered humans before.

Blue had warned him that he might encounter aliens out in the wild. A few even lived in Looking Glass, though Dancer had never seen one in his short stay there. He'd heard plenty of stories. This creature looked like what Blue had called an ael, nomadic scavengers who roamed the far reaches of the northern steppes. They were extremely rare elsewhere on Mirrorworld, solitary and, according to Blue, mute. Some people thought they were natives of Mirrorworld.

"Uh, hello?" Dancer made no sudden moves, just raised his hands, palms facing outward.

The ael sent him a mental image.

Dancer blinked and his mouth dropped open. In his head, he saw himself wrapped mummy-like in his sleeping bag with eyes closed, but from his head, colors flowed, the arc of a rainbow—his dreams made visible. The image vanished after only a moment.

The aels must communicate through telepathy, Dancer thought. Not even Maxwell Blue had guessed that. The ael's psychic communication with Dancer had no verbal component, as it would have had Dancer been hearing from Joah, or Kat. The ael spoke in visual metaphor, a kind of living rebus.

"I don't understand what you're trying to say," Dancer said.

The ael sent the picture again, then one of Dancer sitting up in his sleeping bag with arms extended, mouth wide in a yawn. This picture, too, disappeared after a few seconds. The ael could apparently only string together static pictures. Obviously, though, the alien understood English very well.

"I was asleep, then awake?"

The ael sent a picture of Dancer smiling, though the creature itself never altered its expression.

"Guess I got that one right. Well, um, nice to meet you. I'm Dancer."

The ael responded with a mind picture of the human contorted into

a strange pose and wearing a quizzical expression. Dancer laughed. That was just about what he looked like when he tried to tango.

"Yeah, that's right. Well, actually I'm Daniel Vicksburg. But my friends call me Dancer." He thought of Kat and Joah, and a wave of sadness, and the memories of friendships ripped asunder, struck him. He returned his attention to the ael. "Do you have a name?"

The ael sent an image of the artifact. Dancer blinked. That could mean anything.

"Well, I guess we're not going to do too well with abstracts." Dancer frowned. Back on the other side of the Mirror, he'd gotten some training in the theory of xenolinguistics, just in case the Bugs wanted to talk, but nothing he'd been taught made any sense at the moment. "Do your people even have names?"

Again, the ael sent the image of the green marbled arch.

"Huh. Sorry, but I guess I just don't get it." He shrugged and spread his hands. The ael also made a movement with its shoulders, its first body movement that Dancer had seen, and sent another picture of the arch. "Okay. So, you and this piece of Stonehenge are relatives, huh? How about if I call you Henge? That okay?"

The ael responded with the image of Dancer smiling, but with the rainbow arcing from his skull again. Dancer felt that there might be an emotional subtext as well, but the noise of the artifact was too distracting for him to catch it.

As the sun rose, the song of the stones grew louder. Dancer rolled up his sleeping bag and stowed it hastily. A quick glance at the map that Blue had given him showed that he had wandered far from any marked settlements. Long ago on Earth, they'd had decorated spaces on the maps, labeled "Here there be Dragons," for territory that man hadn't occupied. Mirrorworld maps didn't bother with that little nicety. The settlers were all too aware of the dangers they faced. The maps stuck to geography—in places where the land had been sufficiently explored for the mapmakers to convey that information. Out where Dancer was, there were a lot of blank spaces on those maps.

He figured he needed to get a good distance from the artifact before his mind would be clear enough to concentrate on picking up Joah's trail.

Dancer looked out from the heights he currently occupied into the valley in front of him, and for a moment was disoriented, as always, by just how unimaginably far away the horizon line seemed to be. Maxwell Blue had shown him the trigonometry calculations that proved that Mirrorworld was much larger than Earth, but it was hard to understand the difference until you tried traveling its surface on

foot. An immense blue and emerald forest carpeted the land for many miles around him, perhaps hundreds of miles. Beyond the forest, barely distinguishable in the haze on the horizon, Dancer glimpsed the craggy outline of snow-capped mountains. They must be enormous, he thought.

For a moment, he forgot where he was, even who he was, as he remembered hiking the Rockies with his father and brothers. Those had been good times.

A picture of Dancer bent to climb a mountain pass abruptly flashed across his mind's eye. There was definitely some kind of emotion coupled to the picture, something he almost recognized. He snapped a glance at the ael, a bit annoyed at having his thoughts intruded on. Did this being even understand the concept of privacy?

"I guess you're asking where I'm going?" The smiling face, which Dancer took to be an all purpose affirmative. On impulse, he decided to tell the alien. "I'm on my way to Mere."

Dancer's mind staggered at the next image the creature sent: Dancer, falling off the edge of a mountain. This time, not even the low level roar of the artifact could drown out the powerful emotion of fear beneath the picture. "Why—"

Another image came, of the alien falling with him. Then others, hundreds, thousands of people plunging to their deaths. Terror. Pain. Failure....There was no way to misinterpret the message. Mere represented a terrible danger of some sort.

Dancer studied Henge for a few moments. Where had the ael come from? Why was it interested in him? How was it that it knew about Mere? He shook his head. He had enough to worry about with chasing Joah and Kat. Whoever this alien was, it'd probably be smart to keep his distance. On Mirrorworld, it wasn't safe to trust anyone.

He had a feeling that the alien's appearance here was no accident.

"I'm going now. Nice to have met you." He gave an exaggerated wave, hoisted up his leather backpack with its mahogany frame, and put it on, scooped up his walking stick, and started down the western side of the hill.

Another image formed in Dancer's mind. This one was of Dancer and Henge traveling together toward the mountains. In the distance were the distinct figures of Joah Cray and Kat Fury. Dancer spun around. The ael hadn't moved.

"So, you know about Joah and Kat. Maybe you even picked them out of my head somehow."

Again, Henge sent the image of people falling. Did the ael know

what that image meant to Dancer? His mother had died in a fall during a family hike. He resented the ael's use of that painful memory.

"All right, I get it. You think Mere is dangerous and you know Joah and Kat are trying to go there. But they're my friends, my responsibility. If they have to be stopped, I'm the one who has to do it. Who knows, maybe I'm also the only one who can save them."

Dancer fell silent. He hadn't even admitted that last hope to himself until just now. It felt foolish when spoken aloud. The ael cocked its head slightly, then turned and left the hillside, vanishing in moments. Dancer felt a mixture of relief and loss. He was alone again—just what he'd wanted. But maybe the ael could have helped him....

"I'm sorry," he murmured.

He turned back to the west, his gaze skimming over the ocean of dark green forest before him. How far ahead were Joah and Kat? A few days? A week?

It didn't matter. He would catch them if it took him years. Joah was the brains of the three of them, Kat was the tactician, but Dancer could outrun anyone alive, and he would never give up. They must know that. But what would he do when he caught up to them? How could he stop Joah, short of killing him?

Dancer glanced over his shoulder back at the green stone arch. The sun had risen so that it was now framed by the vertical stones. The artifact seemed to be an ancient window into the eye of a storm of light. He had the fleeting thought that if he looked long enough at it, he might see visions of the past or future.

But he turned away and headed west. He had no use for prophecies.

For him, the past was nothing but pain, and the future seemed likely to be written in blood. Better to run and live only in the present.

◄8 8►

Very soon, Dancer was deep under the forest canopy. Once he had put a few miles between him and the hillside shrine, the sound of its call diminished enough that he could concentrate on tracking Joah. Joah was close, closer than Dancer had expected. For some reason, Kat and Joah were moving much more slowly than usual. Was one of them hurt, or was Joah finally weary of the chase and planning a trap or ambush?

The sun's light filtered through the leaves of the trees, sometimes a subtle green glow, sometimes bright beams that broke through the canopy intermittently to reveal the life of the forest in all its detail. The trees were massive, their trunks many dozens of feet across, their bark gray with age and sometimes completely sheathed in moss. Lichen, thick and pungent, blanketed the rocks on the forest floor.

He saw dozens of different kinds of beetles scuttling over the dead wood of fallen giants, heard birds of all kinds singing, though only rarely did he hear the calls that had thrilled him in his youth back on Earth—one time, he paused to listen in wonder at what sounded precisely like a horned owl.

Dancer stayed off obvious game trails, reasoning that anything big enough to make and use such paths regularly was more than a match for his walking stick and flint pistol. Mostly, he worked hard at moving swiftly and quietly. Blue said that most of the animals on Mirrorworld, including the predators, had little interest in or taste for humans. But there were exceptions.

Dancer paused at a young river to rest, fill his waterskins, and wash his face. The sun dappled the fast moving water. He sat for a moment, mesmerized by the play of light on the water, so bright that it stung his eyes.

As he watched, a craft appeared on the surface of the river, looking a bit like pictures he'd seen of dugout canoes used by South Sea islanders. Figures shifted inside, but he saw them only as silhouettes, black outlines against the forest green of the vegetation on the opposite shore. The shapes were definitely not human. He heard the rush of water against oars and a deep bass rhythmic singing. The canoe passed by him, the rowers' song burring against his ears and thrumming in his chest. He smelled the oil on their bodies as they passed him by; it was the sap from the black and yellow grass.

It was as if he was one with them—his soul flowed out with them and he knew that there was a kind of peace for him there. He need only forget himself for a moment, believe for a fraction of a second in a different flesh, and he might be reborn. He'd have no more regrets, loss, or pain.

The figures in the canoe smoothly changed sides with their oars. The song of their movements beat against the water. These were wedding guardians, sent to one of the four corners of the known world to bar evil from a friend's marriage. Dancer's heart opened to them. Friendship was always, for him, the essence of hope.

He nearly let go of his world to go with them. The temptation was there. Wasn't it possible that he had gone mad long ago, that he was lying strapped to a bed in some institution on Earth, imagining Mirrorworld? Given a choice of dooms, why not join the wedding feast, let go of this hunt that could only end in death?

The canoe glided by and for a glancing moment, he felt the rough wood of an oar in his hands, the warmth of his friends' bodies before and behind him, the smell of a guardian, the taste of spiced wine on his tongue.

Then he blinked and in that instant, the canoe vanished, leaving behind only a momentary echo of an ancient wedding rite.

He rubbed his brow, still staring into the place on the river where the canoe had been. His visions were becoming more vivid. Now he was smelling and hearing them as well as seeing them. Even worse, now they were calling to him.

"Am I going crazy? Is this what happened to Joah?"

The forest gave no answer—just the buzz of insects and the liquid warble of something between a robin and a jay.

With shaking hands, Dancer filled his water bags and washed his face, scrubbing his skin until it stung. Maybe his separation from Joah and Kat was causing this. Or maybe the Triptych Project doctors had damaged his brain, as they must have damaged Joah's when the scientists had made the three of them telepaths. Would he become psychotic like Joah? Was he fated to die alone, insane, impossibly far from home?

Dancer swallowed the water, still chilled from its journey down from the mountains, and stood up. He homed in on his target. Joah's mental signature was like a lodestone to him. Months of practice had made him adept at gauging the distance and direction of his quarry. Joah and Kat had gained a little distance on him while he'd been lost in his fugue state, but not much. For whatever reason, they were slowing down. The two of them were moving at less than half his pace now. He set off once more to find them.

Hours passed and gradually Dancer lost touch with the forest around him in any conscious way. He had sunk into marathoner's mode, moving to the beat of his heart, running when possible, jogging if he had to, but never slowing to a stop. He was in the zone, his muscles warm and working, heart pumping well, lungs drawing deep and free. The heavy pack on his back created a strain in his shoulders and arms, but he was used to that pain and the awkward tilt the weight forced on him to maintain his balance. Twice, he detected snares along the trail and once a cleverly disguised tripwire. But Joah no longer had enough time to set elaborate traps. Dancer was closing the distance.

Above the canopy of the forest, the sun moved slowly across the sky. On Mirrorworld, a day was much longer than on Earth. It made time seem dreamlike, eternal. Dancer's body was sheened with sweat and he

had a headache from straining his eyes and his mind ahead of him, but his legs felt fine and strong. He felt like he could run for hours more.

Sometime after the sun reached its zenith, Dancer arrived at a thinner section of the great forest. Here, the mossy earth changed to rocky grassland, and the predominant species of tree changed to a narrow, white variety that reminded him a bit of Norway pine. These spears of white wood reached high in the sky and terminated in a fan of nude branches that looked very much like the puffball on a dandelion about to consign its seeds into the wind, each tiny voyager carried through the air by a child's breath or a light summer breeze. Finally even those trees thinned out, and he stood at the edge of a breathtaking panorama.

Stretching into the distance behind him, and far away to the north and south, was the vast forest. He had long since passed out of sight of the wild wheat fields and farmlands at the edge of what passed for civilization on Mirrorworld. In front of him, spreading out toward the western horizon, he saw rolling grassland interspersed with clusters of the strange white trees. And, finally, he clearly saw the mountains on

that horizon for the first time. According to his map, he had reached the foothills of the Nabik mountain range.

Now that he was free from the curtain of the forest, it seemed that the mountains he had judged to be so far away were actually quite close, a day's journey at the most. He had badly underestimated their size. These mountains reminded him of the Rockies, blue and black with caps of sparkling snow. The peaks were wreathed in clouds many thousands of feet up. Back in Looking Glass, when travelers had warned him about the Nabiks, he'd discounted their estimates of the heights, assuming they had exaggerated to make the story better. But, if anything, these majestic giants were even more immense than he'd been told. Unless he could find a pass, they were an impossible obstacle, that was certain.

The forest wound around these mountains like the coils of an enormous serpent. His maps showed no trails through the peaks and he wasn't surprised that no one had tried to cross them. If he had a full load of climbing equipment and an experienced team of mountaineers with him, he wouldn't have tried this range without a guide. Even if he was fully prepared, these masters of the Earth would punish anyone who dared to challenge them for the slightest error.

Dancer stood, transfixed. He could smell them, old stone and the hint of snow.

Then, for a moment, the view of the real mountains in front of him wavered, replaced by the sight of a glacier so vast it blotted out the sky before him. Deafening thunder filled the air, punctuated by explosions as the glacier calved, dropping enormous chunks of ice into the valley, each at least the size of a house. The sky around him whirled with the father of all blizzards. Dancer wrapped his arms around his body, assaulted by the sudden freezing cold. A hail began, white chunks of ice hammering at the earth all around him. He threw up his arm to protect his head and, at the same instant, the glacier disappeared.

But Dancer still shivered. A rime of frost speckled his arms and hands. As he watched, disbelieving, it melted away, a victim of the warm day and the heat of his body.

He knelt to the rocky ground, breathing fast, and waited while his heart rate gradually slowed.

"What did you just see, Daniel?"

Dancer looked up. Joah stood there, staring at him with a strange expression that was part amusement, part concern. In the clear daylight, Dancer could more clearly see the filth that covered the other man's animal skins, the scabs and cuts on his face and shaved skull. Around his neck, Joah wore a necklace of bones. At least one of them looked suspiciously like a human finger bone. Had Joah sent that vision of a glacier? Dancer thought he might have. Not all of Joah's traps were physical. That was why he was so dangerous.

"Kat thinks you may be going into dissociative shock." Joah sounded perfectly normal, calm and rational. But his malicious grin told a different story. This was Joah at his most formidable. When he was like this, he was focused—and malevolent.

"What do *you* think, Joah?" Dancer asked.

"I think you may be starting to see things my way."

Dancer felt a spasm of fear. That was his worst nightmare—that he would become the kind of thing his best friend had turned into.

"No."

"You don't sound very convincing, my friend. You were never able to bluff me at poker." Joah smiled. The expression was terrifying on that face.

"I don't want to see what you see," Dancer said.

"Would it be so bad?" Joah replied, dreamily. "You can't imagine the visions I've had, Daniel. Sure, most of them are bloody and cruel, but I've seen some wonderful things, too. I've seen Mere in its childhood, in the days when those mountains were just formed. It's a fantastic place. I think it might be Mirrorworld's Camelot. It still survives, like a diamond hidden in the water. You can't simply walk there, you know…"

"Why are you going there, Joah? What's the point? The Bugs aren't there. And it's the Bugs you're after, right?"

Joah frowned. A cloud of doubt passed through his intense golden eyes. At such times, he looked like a lost, mad child.

"They *were* there…I think." His voice trailed off, and he stared into nothingness. A sliver of saliva trickled from the corner of his mouth. Where was Kat? Joah was only like this when she left him alone for long periods.

"Joah?"

Joah shook his head, glanced to his right, and a sweet, grateful smile transformed his bruised and weary face. Kat must have returned. Joah looked back at Dancer one more time. Without the slightest warning, he whipped out a hand and slapped Dancer hard across his face. The pain was just as real as if Dancer had been physically struck. Dancer still had an ugly scar on his right forearm from the first psychic battle the two had fought. Joah had his own wounds from their many mental battles.

There was no question in Dancer's mind that they could kill each other with their minds. So far, neither of them had tried to be lethal, but Dancer had the feeling that the situation could change at any moment. That thought raised some interesting questions—what if he could defeat Joah on this psychic battleground? Subdue him, or render him unconscious? Might he then be able to make contact with Kat?

The thought galvanized him.

Dancer leapt up and swung his walking stick at Joah, but the other man blocked the blow with a black staff that appeared in his hands. The two exchanged a swift series of blows that ended when Joah retreated several steps. When it came to purely physical contests, even on the psychic plain, the two men were evenly matched.

"Stop following us, Daniel. I don't want to have to kill you."

"Are you sure you can?" Daniel asked.

Joah grinned and disappeared.

It was getting dark and Dancer felt weary—in his mind and spirit as well as in his body. He hiked another mile to a grassy knoll flanked on one side by a stand of the white spear trees. He decided to make camp there. As he took off his backpack, he saw the blackened rocks and scattered ashes of a recent man-made fire. Joah and Kat must have made their camp here, too. Dancer spent a long time just staring at the cold fire pit, with the logs they hadn't burned still stacked neatly beside it.

He went into the woods, gathered up a double armload of slender twigs and sapling for kindling, then went back for some more branches and logs in case he needed to keep the fire going through the night. He hoped this wood wouldn't pop or spit. The white trees looked like hardwood to him, but he couldn't be sure. Nothing on Mirrorworld came with a guarantee. The skill to guess what would burn well and what would fizzle took a long time to acquire—and until Joah's breakdown had broken up their team, Dancer had always left that job to Kat.

Then he scouted the territory around his little camp, checking for traps and snares, and leaving a few tell-tales of his own.

Next he cleaned out the fire pit and constructed a little tepee of thin bits of wood above it. From an inner pocket, he brought out a pouch of tinder. His supply was getting a little low. He should have supplemented it in the forest when he had the chance. At least the fire started easily. By the tremendous heat and the smell of the smoke, he could tell that he might even salvage a few coals to carry with him.

With a sigh, Dancer set about taking care of his chores. First, he took off his boots and studied them very carefully. They'd been custom made for him by a friend of Rain's back in Looking Glass. They were finely made, the stitches so even and tight that they resembled machine sewing. The boots were scuffed, and the right one had a slight tear in one of the lacings, but overall they were holding up well. A good thing. Dancer's father used to say that a hiker was only as good as his shoes. He hadn't been joking. Dancer cleaned the boots, rubbed them with some rendered fat he kept in a little clay jar to waterproof

them and keep them soft, and tapped out some grit that he'd picked up during the day's hike.

Then he took off the rest of his clothes a piece at a time—leather jerkin, wool tunic, silk undershirt and shorts, tough linen pants that fit loosely now on his bony hips, a coat made of something like boiled wool, a double pair of wool socks, and a pair of sheepskin gloves—to check the seams for splits and to clean and brush them before putting them back on. Everything smelled rank from sweat. He wished he had had the time to wash his clothes, or at least take a bath and change his underwear, there at the river. He must smell like something decaying at a landfill. His coat was especially stiff from the sap of that black and yellow grass. One of the arms of the coat had a ragged tear.

As the fire caught hold and died down a bit, he added some more of the small branches he'd gathered, and pulled out his kit and spent some time sewing in the flickering firelight, cursing every time he pricked his thumb with the bone needle. Finally, it was done, though he wouldn't win any prizes for artistry. He set the coat aside, hanging it over a handy branch to air out in the night.

Dancer unlaced his backpack and emptied the contents to inventory his supplies, a depressingly meager store for a man traveling in an unfamiliar wilderness: a bag full of jerky and pemmican that would last him for a few more days, two botas of water filled at the river, a pocketful of acorns and nuts scooped up from the ground cover in the forest, and a bulging pouch of a powder that, when mixed with hot water, made a passable soup. His precious maps were pressed inside a leather flapcase, a gift from Maxwell Blue. The maps were increasingly unreliable, and often useless, now that he was so far off the trade routes. He had a rudimentary first aid kit, silk fishing line with a half dozen bone hooks, a folding camp shovel, and of course his knife and the flintlock pistol. Blue had given him a handmade codex called "Pilgrim's Progress," a compendium of nature lore supposedly collected by the legendary wanderer John Pilgrim. Dancer had committed the whole thing to memory. He never touched any plant that Pilgrim hadn't deemed safe if he could avoid it, and never ate anything that the man hadn't deemed edible.

He had what he needed to survive, but he was acutely aware of what he lacked. He had few tools, no tent, and no spare clothes except for a change of underwear. No compass. As far as he knew, no one had yet worked out a way to make a compass on Mirrorworld. He also didn't have toilet paper. He used handfuls of leaves these days instead. That reminded him that he would have to dig a latrine tonight. He hadn't expected to spend nine months chasing his friends across the world. It was fortunate that they were traveling in Mirrorworld during a relatively mild season. Maxwell claimed that storm seasons on Mirrorworld were so severe that no one left the cities if they could avoid it.

Very soon, Dancer was going to have to start hunting for his food. He wished his friends were with him; Kat was a dead shot with a sling and Joah was a better cook than either Dancer or Kat ever hoped to be.

Dancer unrolled his sleeping bag, wriggled inside and pillowed the back of his head on his crossed hands while staring up at the night sky. He couldn't get used to the brilliance of the stars here, or the sight of two globular clusters where Polaris should have been. Where was this world?

In one sense, Mirrorworld was a fabulous discovery, an Earth-like planet with plenty of space for colonization and no indigenous population other than the aels in the far north, or at least no other population that humans had found in ten years of exploration. If humans had discovered the planet under normal circumstances, they'd probably appreciate the place more. But that wasn't the way it worked out.

One day Mirrors had just appeared on Earth. Nearly everyone who walked through them was stranded on this planet forever. And, back on Earth, death rained from those same Mirrors. The Bugs that obsessed Joah and Kat had come through them one bright Earth morning, killed everything in their path, and vanished. The Bugs had reappeared at intervals—never predictably, and never without wreaking havoc. Nothing had ever been the same for Dancer since—not his life, not his friends, not his home, and—worst of all—not even the person he'd always been. By the time the U.N. had finished with him, he barely knew himself. All he had left was a mission it became clear was futile the day he'd stepped through the Mirror, and a million questions.

There must be answers for them on this planet somewhere. But Mirrorworld was so *vast*. It could take years just to explore a fraction of it. He didn't have years. The way things were going, he couldn't plan his life much past the week it would take for him to catch up to Kat and Joah. He figured, given his odds of surviving that confrontation, planning past that point was a waste of time.

He'd never been too good at being alone, and the loss of his two closest friends, people whose very minds he'd touched, made him feel empty, abandoned, and hopeless. He would have given anything to see the people back in Looking Glass, good people who'd tried hard to make a place for him among them. Right now, he even wished he could see Henge again. The ael was a strange creature, but at least he'd been somebody to talk to.

As Dancer added the remaining logs to the fire, he tried tentatively to reach out with his mind for the ael, and found it surprisingly easy to sense the alien's presence. Too easy.

A vivid image of Dancer standing before the shrine on the hill invaded his mind.

He jerked up to see that Henge was seated cross-legged on the other side of his fire. The alien had its own backpack now, an oval shape with a complicated design of straps. The material looked slick and wet, like leather, or maybe the skin of a snake. The alien looked just as tired and dirty as Dancer felt. He could smell the alien's musky sweat. Henge reeked like a wet dog. Henge had bound a bright blue scarf around his forehead—probably to absorb his sweat—that gave the alien a rakish air. Dancer'd seen something like it once, but the memory slipped away when he tried to access it.

Dancer crawled out of the sleeping bag and put his hand on the hilt of his knife.

"What are you doing here?" He'd meant to sound angry, but the sentence came out only as bewildered and, he had to admit it, a little lonely. It was nice to have something other than the air and a vengeful psychic version of Joah to talk to.

And it was clear the ael meant him no harm. An image flooded Dancer's mind of Dancer and the ael climbing the mountains together.

Dancer took his hand off the knife and stared at the ael. The emotional subtext that had been drowned out on the hillside was crystal clear now in the image he was receiving. The ael was desperate, terribly lonely, frightened, and hopeful Dancer could help him. In fact, Henge's thoughts were so familiar to Dancer that he felt as if he were in contact with Joah, or Kat. But he couldn't respond in kind. Henge's language of images didn't come easily to Dancer. He'd have to stick with human speech, at least until he had a chance to practice Henge's form of communication. Still, Dancer felt a kinship with the ael, an automatic sense that they were alike in some fundamental way.

"You followed me."

<Dancer falling from a great height to an abyss.>

"Yeah, I know it's dangerous. I don't have any choice. But why is it important to you?"

Again, Henge sent the image of the shrine, but it was coupled to something else, a vast arc of color. There were other images in there, too, icons of some sort that Dancer didn't recognize and in some cases couldn't even comprehend. He was reminded of a Dali painting Joah

had shown him once, with ordinary objects warped and melting in a strange landscape.

Henge's emotions coupled to this picture were subtle and alien. Dancer couldn't work them out, though there was definitely a component of danger, the falling sensation.

"Man, I wish you could just tell me what's going on."

Dancer stared down into his fire. As the flames bit through the bark of the big logs into the marrow of the wood, the smoke became tinged with an emerald color and a smell like peat moss filled the air.

It was a vast improvement over his own odor—sweat and grime and that damned rancid butter odor of the grass sap which still covered his clothes and flesh. The new wood was burning well.

Then the image of the fire wavered before him.

Dancer blinked, overcome by a sudden wave of dizziness and nausea. Was this another attack by Joah?

Henge lunged toward him with clawed hands up. Dancer scrambled to his feet, clenched his fists, but he didn't strike. The ael sent a powerfully urgent image of Dancer standing far from the fire, then Henge pointed back to the fire and sent an image of Dancer lying motionless beside it, clutching his throat, looking wretched.

Dancer frowned. The fire…he wavered on his feet, then collapsed. His headache was now much worse and his mouth was dry. Henge pulled his headband down over his face and staggered toward him.

"There's something about the fire," Dancer rasped. "The wood?" He tried to move, and found that he couldn't.

<Dancer smiling, coupled with a powerful echo of the falling sensation.>

Henge grabbed Dancer's collar and dragged him some yards from his camp, out of range of the smoke. Then Henge took a deep breath, and headed back to the fire pit to kick dirt into the flames. The fire died down a bit. Dancer took deep breaths of the cold night air and his head cleared a little, but nausea knotted his gut until he retched. Once he had emptied his stomach, he found he could move again. What was in that wood? Even from yards away, whenever the wind shifted and carried the dregs of the fire's scent to him, it made his head pound and his stomach lurch.

Kat and Joah had left that wood behind for Dancer. If not for Henge's interference, would the smoke have killed him?

"Thanks," he said, shakily, to the ael.

<Dancer smiling.>

There was something else underlying that image as well—some kind of feeling. The ael's emotions were difficult to read. The more adept Dancer became at communicating with the alien, the more textured the feelings he picked up, but paradoxically, the less well he felt he understood the other being. Henge frightened him a little. Why had the alien tracked him over dozens of miles? It didn't make sense. Dancer sighed—Henge had saved his life. Who was he to question a miracle?

As Dancer stared at Henge, the ael clasped its hands over its upper arms and trembled and shook.

Dancer shook his head, but then after a moment got the idea and laughed.

"Right. It's going to be a cold night, unless I make another fire."

<Dancer laughing.>

The ael nodded.

The man shrugged.

"Well, you gotta like somebody with a sense of humor, I guess."

Dancer set to work dousing the rest of the old fire with armloads of dirt, approaching the fire from upwind. He gathered different wood for a new fire a good distance from the old fire pit, silently accepting Henge's suggestions on the choice of kindling and fuel. By the time

the new fire was burning, it was understood between them that Henge would stay. Dancer wasn't sure he trusted the ael completely—there was something off kilter about the alien's feelings, not just his method of communication—but he had to admit it felt good to have a companion. Besides, if the ael meant him harm, why not simply let the fire finish its work?

The two of them cooked meat from their packs, sharing the fire. The smells from Henge's dinner were delicious, something between bacon and garlic. Dancer's dinner smelled like old shoe leather and tasted about the same, but he was too proud to ask for a share of Henge's.

Henge was still awake, staring unblinking into the fire when Dancer finally succumbed to sleep and dreams.

It was a familiar dream, the memory of his first day as a trainee at the UNSP boot camp in Denver.

His brother Jack had driven him to the base and the two men had sat in Jack's car, a battered pickup, listening to jazz on the radio. Dancer's father couldn't get off work and Brian…well, he thought his little brother was nuts and it was better to avoid another fight before one of them said something irrevocable.

"You got the CD?" asked Jack, in his slow drawl.

Everyone in the family wondered where Jack had gotten that drawl, as if he were a changeling from Oklahoma. But it suited Jack, somehow. Jack's long, weathered features with the trademark deepset Vicksburg eyes made him seem like some gunfighter from more than a century ago.

Dancer rustled through his backpack and snatched up the CD of music by John Coltrane.

"Yeah, here it is. Thanks, Jackie."

Jack shrugged and squinted out at the tightly meshed gate that marked off the beginning of miles of camp. A pair of unsmiling guards stood at attention just inside the gatehouse. They were watching the pickup carefully.

"You're gonna do fine, Dancer."

Dancer looked sharply at his eldest brother. Jack never called him Dancer, though everyone else did. For the briefest moment, had he seen a glint of gold in Jack's gray eyes?

"Don't worry, Jack. It's just a couple years. I don't even have to go through the Mirror if I don't want to. A couple years and I'll have enough money for college. I don't know why Brian is so worried."

Jack shrugged again and rubbed his face.

"Well, he's like a sheep dog, y' know. Hates any of his flock to wander."

"I wish he wouldn't keep nipping at me, though," Dancer said. "I'm twenty years old, damn it!"

"Don't worry about it, Dan. Give him a couple weeks to get used to the idea and he'll be fine."

"Dad's okay with this, right?"

"Sure. Well, you know Dad." Jack shifted his eyes to study his younger brother and a sly glint was there. "You know what he said when you called from the testing place?"

Dancer grinned and both men spoke at once.

"'Well, ain't that bright?'"

The two men laughed.

"What do you think Mom would have said?" asked Dancer.

Jack turned away and was silent for a long time.

"Don't give up," he said.

But Dancer didn't like the tone in his brother's voice. There was a hint of something dark there, something that he didn't want to know. Their talk turned to jazz, old gentle arguments about saxophones and singers.

Finally, Dancer got out of the truck and entered the compound, after showing the two burly guards a fistful of papers. He turned once to wave to Jack, who waved back from inside the truck.

He never saw his brother again.

Thanks to Henge, they found a trail through the northern sweep of the forest that flanked the mountains. It appeared to be a marked caravan route, but the path was old and very overgrown. A few minutes on the trail and Dancer knew that they were overtaking Kat and Joah, that they would catch them today, in a few hours perhaps, thanks to the ael.

The trees in this part of the forest had a slick dark bark that glinted as if coated by oil. They had no visible root system, but an enormous number of bright red and green vines and gray runners snaked everywhere on the ground and up above, between the trees. Maybe there was some kind of symbiotic relationship between the vines and trees—the vines got the water, while the trees provided support. The bird calls here were raucous and harsh, and Dancer heard a great deal of activity in the upper branches. Some of it the was the birds, but not all of it. He glimpsed skinny animals scampering among the tree branches. They looked like some kind of cross between chimps and

koalas, and they moved fast. Very fast. He saw one of the creatures actually snatch a colorfully plumed bird right out of the air and begin feasting on it. The successful hunter was soon surrounded by others of its kind, and a screeching battle developed in the forest canopy.

Henge loped ahead of Dancer, leading the way down a path he obviously knew quite well. Dancer, pulling his attention from the battle in the treetops, was content to fix his eyes on the ael and keep up the pace.

For a long while, they were running through a forest fecund with spring—and then, as they ascended, the forest changed. The leaves disappeared from the branches and the path they ran on widened. The ground was covered with a thin crust of snow and Dancer smelled winter in the air. The vines became thin ropes of silver strung between the trees. Dancer was reminded of tinsel on a Christmas tree. The cries of the chimp-koalas and the birds ceased. The forest was peaceful except for the stirring of the barren branches as they moved in the wind—a dry, sibilant reminder of the winter that still gripped the heights, and a promise of worse to come as they climbed.

One moment, Dancer heard only the slap of his boots against the packed earth, muffled by the snow; the next he was surrounded by a caravan of aels on some unguessable journey. He still saw Henge ahead of him, but very soon the ael disappeared ahead of him into the crowd of his kind. Henge never paused.

The caravan reminded Dancer of the wagon trains he'd read about in Earth history books. The aels had a score of wagons, each constructed around one massive axle turning a pair of gigantic spherical wooden wheels. The wagons were guarded by hosts of aels bearing what looked like staff slings. The staffs were tipped with clusters of small green bells that tinkled rhythmically as the aels walked. The guards wore white vests and kilts, and the tops of their boots were tied around their calves by intricately knotted ribbons. These aels were very tall, much taller than Henge, and their hair was a dazzling white. Were these females, or males, or did the aels have genders? Who could tell? Nobody in Looking Glass knew much about the aels, let alone how to tell the sexes apart, or if they even had two—or more—separate sexes. Dancer didn't see any children anywhere, though he supposed they might be inside the massive wagons.

Dancer stopped running. He couldn't run in this crowd anyway.

Creatures in the caravan, beasts of burden that looked vaguely bird-like, trotted along with a weird splay-footed gait. He heard the aels' voices, smelled their cooking, brushed against their pelts, wiry and coarse. He couldn't stop staring at them, nor could he ignore the very real feeling that he was welcome here. As with the wedding guardians in the canoe, he knew that he need only open his mind—now obsessed with a purpose he no longer understood—to become part of this forever, part of a new and cleaner life.

He looked down at his hands. They were, oddly enough, covered in white fur. His vision had changed, too. His eyes seemed to see more clearly, though the scope of what he saw was narrower. And those were just the smallest symptoms of the massive change that gripped him. A thousand differences in the mesh and flow of his body were falling into place now, as if his soul were the note of a tuning fork gradually changing pitch.

"Where are we going?" But he knew.

"Mere," said a quiet voice with a hint of a warble in it.

Dancer looked to his left and Henge stared back, now kin who could speak to him, of course. Henge's slitted eyes were dark, and for the first time Dancer noticed that the bony ridges that defined the ael's skull were soft and supple, not rigid as he'd originally thought. Henge still wore his bright blue head scarf, the one that seemed somehow familiar.

"You can speak," Dancer said.

"Here. Then." The ael's face changed, but Dancer was helpless to

understand what this new expression might mean. Certainly, the alien's voice revealed no emotion that Dancer could interpret. There was a strong psychic undercurrent passed to the human, a sense of dread, the awful falling sensation. But wasn't there something else woven in there as well, some hint of joy barely disguised?

"Please, tell me what's happening to me," Dancer begged.

"Mere," the ael said.

"I don't understand."

"We are called. We answer."

In that reply, and the serene resignation beneath it, Dancer understood something crucial about the ael. *We're so much alike,* he thought.

"Who is calling us?" He stared at the ael. "If it's Mere, then how, why?"

The ael was silent for some time, but Dancer was learning a little how to interpret Henge's moods and he thought that the alien was not so much reluctant to speak as at a loss for words.

"Well, can you at least tell me what this caravan is?" asked Dancer.

The ael's expression changed minutely, but Dancer's evolving perceptions made it comprehensible. The ael was glad to be here.

"There are Roads," said Henge, "that lead to moments. Here, now, is the Road I traveled in my youth to Mere."

"You were a pilgrim, then?"

The ael's slitted eyes widened slightly, which could mean either surprise or anger among the aels. Dancer wasn't attuned enough to know for certain which. Certainly, there was no great change in Henge's voice.

"'Pilgrim'? Mere is not God. Our journey is a thread of the Now."

"The 'Now'?"

Dancer stopped abruptly and Henge paused, too. He had the feeling that the two of them were finally touching the heart of the matter.

"Our souls live in the Now, our bodies trapped in Then and Perhaps. You and I have met by Mere's design, though your friend Joah believes he is the master planner."

"But why are you here? Why did you seek me out? How did you know to find me?"

"Mere. My friend, I know only one answer. I am chosen out of the Now to guide you, as you are chosen. Surely, you understand? "

The trouble was, he did understand, inchoately. As Dancer became more entwined with the life of this caravan—this strange, endless journey—he found it harder to differentiate his thoughts from

Henge's, to formulate a question in human terms. The problem was time…Henge's people had little conception of it as a delineating concept. For the aels, planning ahead was more a matter of instinct then cognition.

Very soon, if he remained here, he would become a part of this caravan, this Now. He already felt more complete here. It was very similar to the feeling that he had when he was with Joah and Kat, a sense of multiplicity and harmony. It was almost the music of fate, but no…the answer was both ineffable and elegant, if he could only stay here a little longer to experience it, to understand.

"You must leave," said Henge.

But Dancer was not listening to the ael. There was some sort of music in the air. Yes, some of the aels in the caravan had donned purple garments, like fringed scarves, and brought out an assortment of musical instruments. As they played, they improvised with the melodies of a thousand times a thousand other caravans. It was jazz taken to some ultimate place.

"Do you hear?" he murmured. Oh, what Jack wouldn't have given to be with him at this moment. But *wasn't* he here? Of course he was. *We are all here, now, somewhere along the Road.*

"Dancer! You can only aid Mere as a human."

The ael put one of its bony, wickedly clawed hands on his shoulder, but Dancer didn't move. The words made no sense. This was no place for words. This Road was for music and thought and…yes!…memory.

"I think I understand. We are called. We—"

But then Henge did something. Dancer felt the wrench in his gut and his mind. The ael had shifted them somehow, to a different moment of the Now. But why? Just as they were becoming one—

Dancer's nascent comprehension slipped from his mind as if it were quicksilver through his fingers. Something about memory. Mere reaches out, but can also be called? Dancer clenched his fists. So close, but the ael had pulled him away. Henge was gone, as if the ael had never been. But the vision of the caravan to Mere remained. But now, Dancer wasn't a matched companion. Something was out of joint. It sounded in his mind as if all the instruments of the aels were abruptly mistuned, misplayed.

The caravan continued on, while the seasons continued to wheel around them, but now with frenetic movements, a jangle of darkness. Soon, they were moving through summer and all the aels had hair tinted dark brown, black, and red. There was a different feeling now, a dread of doom. This was a new thread of the Now and Dancer knew

instinctively that it was somehow his fault, that he had failed Mere in its moment of need. He felt terribly ashamed.

The caravan paused. A furious sound like the whispering of a god filled the air. It was a whisper he had heard before. Dancer stared up into the sky and watched with horror as flying creatures descended out of the sky. The picnic dream! But was that really a dream? These creatures falling out of the air like spears from the sun weren't Bugs…exactly. But—

Dancer heard a soft whuffing sound that made his ears ring. The earth shifted beneath his feet as if someone hammered it from below. The vibration knocked him to his hands and knees. When he looked up, the caravan was gone, the chance for him to join that infinite journey was lost. He was back in the spring of Mirrorworld, and the screams of the animals and birds were deafening.

The ground trembled for what seemed hours, though he knew it could only be seconds. Then all the world fell strangely silent, as if the forest itself were holding its breath. The sky darkened and Dancer smelled smoke. Soon, smoke filled the air everywhere and he was standing in a grey cloud of it, unable to see the path in front of him. He felt as if someone was pouring salt on him, and his hands and face began to sting.

When he brought his hands close to his face, he smelled ash and cinders mixed with the rancid butter odor that he'd become more or less used to in the last few days.

Ash? Cinders?

Then he heard the explosions, and the smell of fire filled the air. The mountains—could this be a volcano erupting? He stood frozen for a moment. The cloud of ash was so thick that he could barely see his own hands. He certainly couldn't see Henge, if the ael was still here. For a moment, he was confused about what direction he'd come from. He was trapped in a forest fire, maybe even a volcanic eruption. Should he go forward or back? Would either direction save him?

Then the heavens rained fire. Fragments of flaming wood dropped from the sky like fiery comets to explode all around him. Those could be lava bombs, or the exploding fragments of high resin trees caught in a forest fire. Either way, if they were falling this close to him, then he was a dead man.

Dancer stood there uncertainly for a moment longer, then an image appeared before him. It was a beautiful woman with Eurasian features and long black hair. She wore clothing made from animal skins, and had some kind of leather gloves on her hands.

Kat!

She looked at Dancer and smiled, but it was a strained smile and she kept glancing to her right. She seemed to be holding some sort of conversation with someone. The corners of her eyes crinkled as she squinted. Dancer knew that meant she was furious. Was she arguing with Joah? There was no way he could tell—not that it mattered to him at this moment when death was so near. But after a brief interlude, she turned again to Dancer and beckoned to him to follow. Dancer hesitated only for a moment. What did he have to lose, really? He would rather die trusting Kat than die alone. He bent over—the air was better closer to the ground—and followed.

Kat's image led him on through the smoke and flaming patches of vegetation for what seemed like miles, but was probably a few hundred feet. Very soon, he realized that they were moving closer to the fire, and again he hesitated. But Kat looked back and smiled at him, that crooked half grin that she always used when she thought he was being silly. After that, he didn't pause, but ran along behind her.

They came at last to a wall of flame whose heat beat at his skin, though not as painfully as he expected. All around him, trees were exploding and the roar of flames filled the air. He was truly trapped. Kat glanced back at him and mouthed three words. Dancer thought that she might say something more, but then she vanished.

Dancer stood a moment longer outside the wall of fire. If Kat had betrayed him, then he was dead. Here and now, he was faced with the real reason he'd chased his two friends for all these months. It wasn't to protect Mirrorworld from Joah. It wasn't even because he thought that Joah could save him from the visions.

He had followed them because he had to see Kat again. He had to know what was really in her heart. Covering his head with his arms, Dancer rushed toward the flames as fast as he could run, repeating the whole time the three words she'd mimed for him—"Ain't this bright?"

He covered his face with his wool coat, damp with his sweat, and leapt as high as he could into the curtain of fire. He felt a flash of suffocating heat and terror, then he passed safely through the flames. The leading edge of the forest fire had stalled here, where a rocky, barren plain led to a series of foothills below the mountains. With nothing to burn for hundreds of yards, the greedy fire was faltering, running out of fuel. The smell of his own singed hair filled his nostrils, so he beat at his hair with his coat—if his hair was burning, the damp wool would smother the flames. He crawled across the uneven surface of the plain until the heat behind him was no longer so intense, then he couldn't feel it at all. The air was clear at last. Some of the smoke from the fire had gotten into his lungs, but he was otherwise unharmed.

He stopped for a moment, all bent over, and coughed until his breathing eased. Finally, he stood up and staggered onward.

Dancer stumbled as far as he could from the edge of the blazing forest. He scrambled over the rocks, paying no attention to the ash that continued to fall around him or the numerous coals and embers that littered the ground beneath him.

Some time later—he couldn't have said how long, though it seemed like many hours—he felt he had climbed far enough away from the fire to be out of immediate peril. He turned back to look at the forest. The light of the flames was so bright that it turned the night sky into a scarlet banner. The sky was black with clouds of smoke as far as he could see in any direction. The fire raged over the ancient forests. It was like looking at an old-fashioned painting of Hell. Hundreds of thousands of acres of forest were burning, and they would keep burning for who knew how long. For certain, this part of the world would be impassable for a long time to come.

Dancer reached out with his mind. He could sense Joah's mental signature, oddly muddled at the moment, but distinctive. There could be no mistake; he was on the other side of that burning forest, and the

link was getting weaker every moment. Soon, they would be cut off for good. Dancer wouldn't be able to track Joah any further for now. It would take him days, maybe even weeks, to find a way around this mess. The chase was over for the time being.

Dancer sprawled against an outcrop and just stared, almost uncomprehending, at the inferno. It was a miracle he'd made it out of there alive. He looked down at his arms and saw that a fine sooty powder covered his flesh. He wiped at it absently, gradually uncovering his skin in a few small patches. When he did, however, the heat of the flames seemed suddenly to find him in those places, and his skin blistered there within moments. He hurriedly coated his exposed flesh with some of the soot from the rest of his arm. As he did so, he realized that the soot was mixed in with the sour sap of the grass that he'd been traveling through for all these months.

The sap. It must have insulated his skin from the fire.

Dancer tried to laugh, but his throat, raw from coughing and smoke inhalation, felt as if it were being jabbed with broken glass. He hacked a bit, then gave it up. After all that misery, after all of his griping, after smelling that horrible rancid butter stench until it made him want to puke, the nasty stuff had finally proved useful. In fact, it had probably saved his life. It was ironic—the bath he'd regretted not taking might have killed him if he'd had it. He kept moving, until even his burned flesh believed that the air was cool, until only the scarlet sky behind him and a faint tinge of smoke on the breeze gave any indication of the fate he'd barely escaped.

Dancer spread out his sleeping bag—now badly scorched in places and leaking feathers, but he was too tired to care—and stretched out, intending only to rest for a moment. Exhaustion and the fear that he would never see Joah and Kat again sapped what little strength he had left.

Despite his intentions, he sank into a deep sleep. As always, his memories came back to haunt him in his dreams.

◄8 8►

Dancer sat at a card table in a room lit by half a dozen scented candles. To his left was Kat. She was wearing her Oxford sweater and the green tinted glasses that made her look like something out of a Beatles movie. To his right, Joah Cray was shuffling a deck of cards. In the center of the table was a pile of poker chips.

"Five card stud, nothing wild, Bugs to open," said Joah.

Kat laughed and Dancer stared at his friend. He'd forgotten that Joah used to have a light voice and a quick sense of humor.

"Daniel, are you in or out?" asked Joah, his eyes lambent in the candlelight.

Those eyes…since the biotrooper enhancements, since the Triptych treatments…Joah's eyes had changed. They generated some kind of bioluminescence now. It was weird, a little frightening. But it was still Joah in there. Right?

<In or out, my friend?>

The telepathic message caught him by surprise. It was incredible! He could hear the words in his head, but there was also a, well, a pool of some sort around the words, a pool of intention. He could sense Joah's innocent pleasure at surprising him, could feel the man's strength and warmth.

The moment shifted abruptly in Dancer's mind to a night not long after. Joah was poised at the Mirror. Kat was unconscious in his arms. Were the guards dead?

"No, Joah. Don't do this."

<In or out?> Joah's thoughts were tinged with white hot fury, but also a hint of sorrow, of need.

<Leave Kat.>

<Don't follow us.>

Joah leapt into the Mirror and the severing of their mental bond was an explosion in Dancer's head. Dancer hesitated, but he'd felt Kat's mind stirring at the moment of Joah's escape. She'd called out for him. Dancer looked once around, looked up into the sky. Was this the last time he'd see the stars of Earth? Then he stepped through the Mirror, into madness.

Again, in that seamless way that dreams have of abandoning one reality for the next, the scene shifted to a bridge in Looking Glass. It was many months later, as he, Rain, and Maxwell Blue all stood in a tower looking down on the devastation of the city of Looking Glass. If not for an unseasonable rain, the city might have been entirely destroyed by fire. As it was, Father's bomb, planted—unwittingly?—by Kat and Joah had crippled so much. The library was almost entirely destroyed, all those precious books, most of them irreplaceable, were forever gone. Fire had destroyed most of the Gray Quarter where hospitals and schools once stood.

"Father will attack with the light," said Rain. A very tall muscular black woman, Rain was a legend in the biotrooper program. Dancer still couldn't quite get used to knowing her. "Will you stay, Dancer? Are you in, or out?"

Dancer was desperate to continue his chase—none of them, not even Blue, really understood how close to insanity separation from Kat and

Joah was bringing him—but how could he refuse? One of his triptych had to pay this bill. He nodded. Rain said nothing more, but he got the feeling that she despised him slightly less. She was a hard woman. Then Dancer thought of the dead and maimed people, many of them her friends, down there in the city, and couldn't really blame her.

"The truth, Dancer," asked Blue, quietly. "Do you think the two of them knew what was in that shipment of books?"

Rain didn't look at them, or even seem to be paying attention, but her grip on the railing was tight.

"I don't know, Max," said Dancer. "I hope not."

Blue started to say something else, but a voice interrupted him.

"Of course we knew."

Dancer spun around. Joah leaned there, partly hidden in shadow. His eyes burned in the darkness, like reflections of the fires below. Joah had removed some essential disguise. He must always have had access to Dancer's memories and dreams, but now that the chase had ended, he no longer bothered to hide it, or his guilt for the mess back in Looking Glass.

"Why, Joah?"

"Isn't it obvious? Father had a map to Mere and Mere is the key to the Bugs on Mirrorworld. Mere is the key to a lot of things. It was a simple trade."

The tower and bridge and Looking Glass itself wavered out of focus, out of Dancer's memory. The two of them were now standing in a field cloaked in darkness. He stared at his friend with horror.

"Dear God. You killed all those people…for a map to a place that doesn't exist?"

Joah's expression didn't change.

"We're soldiers, Daniel, and this is war. Civilized rules don't apply. The key to finding the Bugs is in Mere. I'd do anything for that key."

Dancer slumped down, wrapped his long arms around his legs.

"All those people…They were just trying to make some kind of life here. You're a murderer, Joah." Dancer looked up, tears in his eyes. He could hardly bear to go on. But he had to ask the next question, the one he most dreaded. "Did Kat know?"

"Why don't you ask her?"

Joah gestured and there she was, her presence in the link like a torrent of wine to a man who had thirsted so long he'd forgotten the taste of water. The link was complete, the triptych circuit in place. With Joah acting as bridge, they could communicate easily now. Was this a final gift, of sorts, a gesture of friendship, or another of Joah's tricks?

"Kat?"

She met his gaze and, as if her eyes truly were windows into her soul, he understood at once that the memory of the picnic was Kat's. She didn't need to speak. The black pearl of rage she had nourished was plain in her mind.

The two of them faded away and gradually Dancer realized where he was standing—a cemetery. Many of the headstones were marked with the carved icon of a Bug.

The Village of Ghosts

Dancer woke with the dawn. Fitful gray light filtered through the clouds blanketing the sky. Every muscle in his body ached, the burns on his arm stung, and he felt too tired to move. Fires burned far below, and he spent some time just staring as the flames raced across the ancient forest. He had never seen anything like it. Maybe in the earliest days of Earth, when humans had just begun to comprehend their existence, men had witnessed such fires. Then the conflagrations must have seemed like the end of the world, as their source of food and shelter was consumed by an endless, trackless world of flame. Ash continued to rain down from the sky and the air was choked with the smell of sulfur. Dancer wondered what had started the fire—if, as seemed likely from the rain of ash, it was a volcano, then he wondered where the eruption had occurred and what its magnitude was. If this was the aftermath of a Vesuvius, the world would limp onward, bruised in places, but not truly altered. If this was a Tambora-level eruption, then Mirrorworld itself might be permanently maimed.

The earthquake and the fires that had accompanied the eruption weren't that terrible in the global scheme of things—but the possibility that the volcano's emissions might screen out the sun for months was. If the eruption was serious enough, if the clouds of ash and steam were tossed high enough and for long enough, mass extinctions would surely follow. The climate would change, temperatures drop, and the fragile presence of man on this new world would end. He didn't know how bad this was—Mirrorworld didn't have CNN. He could only wait and see. In fact, there was nothing Dancer could do about it right now—except survive.

Dancer reached out for Henge, but the ael's odd mental signature was also gone. Dancer felt a terrible grief. The ael had probably perished in the fire. If it hadn't been for Kat, Dancer would never have found his way out. They had been so close to understanding everything about one another, until the ael shifted him into that disastrous moment that shattered the Road. The worst of it was that Dancer had the unshakeable feeling that he, himself, was responsible for that destruction, or at least complicit in the ending of that infinite joyous journey. His eyes were wet, but only partly from the sting of hot air and swirling ash.

Joah appeared before him.

"We're on the other side of the forest, Dancer. You'll never catch us now."

"It wouldn't matter if you were on the other side of the world, Joah. I'll find you. I'll never stop hunting you."

"You've lost, Dancer. Why not accept it?"

Dancer faced his old friend, his bitter enemy.

"You know me better than that, Joah. I can't leave you out there. You're too dangerous. What if you did find the Bugs, anyway? You're just as likely to draw genocide down on every living thing on Mirror-world as anything else."

Joah gave a thin smile.

"What would you say if I told you that I didn't care?"

"I don't believe you."

"I would do anything to destroy the Bugs. Anything. If it takes the death of every living thing on Mirrorworld for me to learn one important fact about the Bugs, so be it."

Dancer stared at his friend, at those glowing golden eyes. He'd never been able to tell when Joah was bluffing. Could he be serious about this? He spoke of the deaths of a world full of people as if they were no more than counters on a game board. How was he able to hide this from Kat? Or, God, did she agree with him?

"I can't let you do that, Joah."

Dancer lifted his walking stick. Though they had battled often, hurt each other often—sometime severely—he hadn't tried to kill Joah before on this psychic plane. He'd always hoped to find a way to save him, to heal his mind. But now...well, Dancer had never cared that much about the Bugs. It was the innocents of this world that mattered to him. The time had come, the instant that he had dreaded from the moment he'd followed Joah through the Mirror.

"Let's put an end to it, Joah. Here and now."

But Joah didn't immediately join the fight. In fact, he looked lost and sad.

"Kat would never forgive me." His voice sounded bleak. "If only you could see what I see, you'd join us. The Bugs threaten everything, not just this one world. Why can't you see that?"

"It's not up to me to stop the Bugs. I'm concerned with those kids back in Looking Glass who were maimed and killed by your obsession. I'm sorry, Joah. Only one of us can leave here alive."

Joah nodded. He didn't look particularly concerned, but then he was a master poker player. They both knew that in physical contests, Dancer had the edge.

"There's something you're forgetting, Daniel."

"What's that?"

"If you kill me, what's to prevent you from becoming me? You've started having the visions, haven't you? You're being led to Mere, just as Kat and I were. You're doomed, my friend."

Dancer hesitated. Could Joah be right?

"I'll just have to take that chance." He stepped forward, preparing to strike, but Joah didn't move.

"What if there was another way, for both of us?"

Dancer lowered his staff, fractionally. It was a trick; it must be.

"What do you mean?"

"It's the separation of the triptych that's causing our psychosis," said Joah. "If you joined with me, we could work together to heal the breach."

Dancer was tempted. Hadn't he secretly hoped for this very chance? But there was a flaw in Joah's logic and he saw it immediately.

"If it's the separation that's caused your madness, how do you explain your trip through the Mirror, the dead guards?"

"What are you talking about, Daniel?" Joah looked honestly puzzled. "That never happened. We went through the Mirror together, as a team."

For a moment, a very brief moment, the entire structure of Dancer's mind shuddered. Could it be true? From the beginning, hadn't he felt an odd disconnection with his memories, as if they were somehow mutable? Dancer frowned. Ever since he'd met Henge, in fact, his identity and memory had become frighteningly fluid.

"Your memory isn't what it used to be, is it?" asked Joah, softly, guessing exactly what Dancer was thinking. "There's no hope for either of us, Daniel, unless we work together, unless we join minds."

Could it be? The idea that he might become as psychotic as Joah terrified him. What if he ended up killing people, too? What if he hurt Kat? But how could he trust Joah?

"I know you don't trust me, Daniel. But please believe me. This may be the last chance for all three of us." Joah tossed away his own staff and spread his hands. "Here I am. Go ahead and strike. Maybe you're right. Maybe I should be dead."

Dancer stepped closer. Joah made no move to defend himself. This close, he saw the stubble on his friend's cheeks, the lines at the corners of his eyes and mouth, the bristles of new hair beginning to speckle the shaved skull. Joah smiled gently and closed his strange glowing eyes and waited. Dancer lifted the staff. It was a trick. It must be. He lowered the staff slowly to his side. But what if it wasn't?

"All right," Dancer whispered. "We'll try the meld."

He opened his mind to Joah, but kept his mental defenses up. Joah also opened a door into his mind, but every wall was down. Dancer could see the way into the depths of Joah's psyche. It was a glittering corridor. He had left himself completely open, both physically and psychically. Dancer hesitated for another moment, then dove deep into Joah's mind.

He fell through that shining corridor, which for Dancer was a metaphor for Joah's complex and brilliant mind, and found himself caught in a maelstrom of such thunderous madness that there was no hope that he would ever be able to meld with it. Joah knew. It was a trap, but one that neither could escape.

Dancer descended into Joah's madness.

◄8 8►

He was a child, lost in a blindness filled with awful sounds. There was a humming of bees, screaming, broken cries, a crack like tiny lightning. He heard the crying, sobbing so hopeless that it made him want to scream out with terror.

There was pain, an endless maze of it and it was central to the child-Joah. He had names for all the many hurts.

The blindness lifted for a moment to reveal a woman's bleeding and broken body crawling away from a door. A shadowy figure filled the doorway. The sound of bees. The crack of lightning. Pain. The immense figure became a vision of a Bug so vivid that he cried out.

A forest of trees so gigantic that he couldn't see their tops. The bark was shifting before his eyes, becoming smooth, becoming skin, scabbed and hairy. The buzzing of bees. The many-named hurts. The shadowy figure of a man.

He was older now, sight cracked like a shattered windshield. In each fracture, a different image of memory and possible memory unwound. In many of the fragments, a woman is beaten. In others, a man removes a silver-buckled belt and lowers a zipper, which makes a sound like buzzing bees.

The pain, the shame, the guilt, the horror…he calls them the Bugs.

Daniel relived Joah's life, over and over and over…until one day, the boy ran away, leaving a broken mother. He ran away to kill the Bugs.

When Dancer woke, he opened his eyes and saw the world shattered into fragments. Joah was gone, long gone, beyond the reach of his mind. But his legacy remained. The buzzing of bees.

Dancer wept, screamed until he was hoarse, but the nightmare memories remained and the world was fractured in his sight. In one fragment, the dead of Looking Glass, in another a naked woman who touched his body and mind, were the only barriers between him and absolute insanity. In some of the jagged windows, Dancer glimpsed what must be Joah's vision of Mere, a strange discordant jumble of images and ideas. In many of the fragments, Dancer's visage was clear, a clean and honest truth that Joah clung to, desperately. There were too many facets, all constantly changing, blurring, then burning with clarity.

He couldn't stop hearing the buzzing of the bees.

But gradually, like climbing a vertical rock face, Dancer struggled to fuse the Dancer facets into one clear window. It was painstaking work, performed in the dark, by an instinct that he knew was partly Joah's own crude technique, learned from childhood. Poor Joah. He had always seen the world this way, a fractured window. Dear God.

How long he remained near-catatonic, Dancer couldn't imagine.
But there came a time when the Dancer-window was large enough. He
could see out of it. He had learned to let the focus of the other windows
blur, though it gave him an evil headache. The buzzing sound of bees,
which was both pain and fear, couldn't be silenced, but he could move
again, he could think and act.

Joah lived in this fragmented world. Dancer still couldn't imagine how.

Dancer stared down at the tapestry of fire in the valley, still burning
far below. His eyes were like those of an insect. Dozens of repetitions of
the fire reflected and burned in his mind. Some of the fires were…
different, memories or possibilities. It was terrifying, but also fascinating.
He stared and dreamed and continued to fuse his mental window, to
make it clearer. Was this how he must live the rest of his life? How
could Joah have ever lived at all, like this? Did Kat know?

Dancer watched the spread of the fire. He saw the Road burn. He
fought the urge to unblur those other hideous windows, some of them
merged with Mere itself. If he let himself wander now, he was lost.

Grimly, just as if he were running the longest marathon of his life,
Dancer worked on his window into reality. Just a little more, he
thought. But the buzzing…the laughter of his father as he unzipped
his pants…the Bugs…

Hunger and thirst eventually drove him from his perch. The clouds in
the air had thinned a bit and the sun found gaps to warm the earth. He
climbed up the slope in front of him to a flat passage through the
foothills. Very soon, he found a mountain pool fed by a waterfall. On this
end of the lake, its smooth surface was coated with a drift of gray ash.

He stripped off all his clothes and dove into the pool. The shock of
the frigid water against his bare skin made him gasp, nearly made him
stop breathing. Hadn't he read somewhere that freezing water could
stop a heart? But his beat on. In his new, fractured sight, the pool
became multiple pools, too many to count. One blurred window
showed a tantalizing fragment of a bowl, filled with scented water and
birds. It felt as if it might be a vision of Mere. If only he could see it
clearly, but he dared not look too closely. The master window, the
opening into reality that Dancer had made, was too fragile. The other
fractures were too sensitive to his mood. If he let his mind wander, even
a bit, he would be lost again in Joah's reality.

He swam until his body became used to the temperature of the water.

The he settled in a shallow pool that the sun had warmed and used the silt from its bottom to scrub away at his body. The rancid grease from the weeds, the dirt from weeks on the trail, the scent and texture of a life spent too long in the wild took a long time to get off his skin. As he scrubbed, old scabs broke open and new scrapes and muscle aches twinged. He welcomed the pain. It was a relief from the odd numbness that seemed to surround his thoughts.

Dancer scrubbed his clothes, too, as well as he could. The smell of the sap, mixed with soot, fire, and sweat was so embedded in everything he owned that he knew it would never really fade. His boots worried him most. They'd been damaged by the fire. He might get a few more good weeks of walking out of them, but pretty soon he'd have to get new ones, or make them. He had a hazy idea of how to go about making boots from animal skins, but he didn't have the tools for doing it.

Dancer shrugged. He couldn't seem to care. It was as if he were half awake now. His thoughts were jumbled and slow, and his emotions muffled. He had to make a plan, had to return to the hunt. Joah must be stopped. There was no doubt in Dancer any more. Joah was insane. He could pity the man, understand what had overthrown his reason, but now he knew the truth. The only thing keeping Joah alive was that window with Kat in it.

Naked, Dancer spread out his clothes to dry on a line he tied between two trees. He set a small fire under the wool garments—it was the only way they'd dry any time in the next millennium. He stood for a moment as he waited to see if the fire would take. It did. Soon the wool was gently steaming in the fire's smoke as the coat dried. Ash was still falling intermittently as the wind shifted. He sat on a rock to wait for nature to take its course with him and his garments. He let his eyes half close, as rays of sunlight and the occasional silken kisses of a mountain's rage brushed his skin. The clouds in the air had parted sufficiently to let a little of the sun shine down, but even so the air was still cold. At least the little valley shielded him from the wind. He pulled his sleeping bag from the pack, and wrapped it around himself.

Half asleep, Dancer felt something caressing his mind. It felt as if a dove were beating her wings, on the verge of taking flight, and the feathers were just brushing his skin—ever so lightly. The sensation was odd, but pleasant and somehow familiar.

After some time, he frowned, stood up, and concentrated on locating the source of the feeling. It seemed nearby, though not close in any physical sense.

Dancer put on his clothes, though they were still slightly damp, banked the fire, packed his gear, shouldered his pack, and wandered through the bowl-shaped clearing. He guessed that he was in a depression gouged out by a glacier sometime in the distant past. There were slopes all around him that led up into the foothills, and foothills that led into the heart of the mountains.

Joah and Kat were on the far side of this forest fire. He had lost their mental signatures and it would take months for the fire to burn itself out. No matter. He'd go around. It had taken nine months to track and almost catch them. If it took nine more months, or nine years, Dancer would spend it. Joah Cray had to be stopped…face it, killed. There was no way to heal those windows, those memories. Dancer saw that now. Joah had wanted him to see, to understand.

It was strange to be unable to find out anything about the disaster. Back on Earth, news reports of such catastrophes were broadcast around the world in minutes; sometimes disasters were even predicted, like the Mount St. Helens blasts back in the twentieth century. Here on Mirror-world, nothing was known for certain. Everything was mysterious, unpredictable. Was it any wonder that biotrooper tyrants like Father were so necessary to the fearful and the confused people of this planet? Father was absolutely sure of everything. Even if he killed them, he offered his people answers. Dancer, Rain, Blue, and the rest of them had no answers.

Thinking of Father reminded Dancer of Joah and Kat. Joah had answers, too. What was it about this place? The only folks with a concrete plan seemed to be sociopaths. He pushed the thought out of his mind. Dancer kept walking, seeking the source of that gentle mental touch.

Occasionally, images of objects and people flashed before Dancer. He heard voices talking. Sometimes he recognized them, but mostly they were unfamiliar. These were only a minor annoyance. Some of them were whispering from Joah's facets, others from Dancer's own.

Dancer let his thoughts drift as he wandered through the clearing, searching for the source of the caress he could still feel against his mind. Finally, he came to a part of the clearing where the sound of whispering was louder, clearer.

He followed his instinct down a natural funnel of stone to a trench of old rock. It looked something like a winding river filled with all sorts of different stones. In his mind's eye, in one of the multitude of memory mirrors, he saw the trench flowing with ice. A roar of stones cracking and tumbling filled his ears.

He shook his head, focused his sight through his own clearest window, and the vision disappeared. He picked his way carefully to the bank of the dead river. Twice, his ankle nearly turned as he slid over loose gravel, pinwheeling his arms in a desperate search for balance. Each time he stopped and checked his feet inside the heavy leather boots. No pain or swelling, and his joints moved freely. The two close calls sobered him and made him more cautious in his movements.

If he fell here, broke an arm or leg, he'd die, no two ways about it. He had little food and water, and absolutely no hope of help. A small part of him sighed with relief at the thought of a peaceful death, of just laying down the burdens of his life and drifting off. It was tempting, and survival was so hard.

On the other hand, the UN School back on Earth had taught its students very well what dying of starvation and thirst was like. There were a lot of better ways to die. Dancer kept walking.

On the edge of the ancient riverbank, Dancer crouched down and squinted at a jumble of green stones in the bed of the dry river. They were odd, no question about it. At first, he thought they must be covered with some kind of lichen, but his closer inspection revealed that these stones were veined with the same chips of green that he'd seen in the tori of the stone arches where he'd first met Henge.

The stones were calling to him, purring to him like stone kittens. He reached out a tentative hand and stroked one of the rocks and its murmur shifted, from gentle caress to something lower and stronger.

"What's this?" he said.

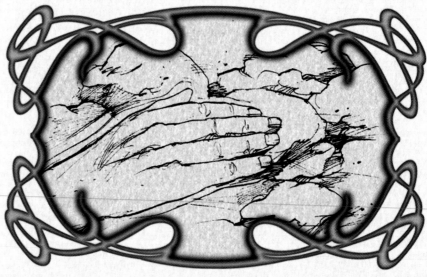

His voice came out as a croak. His throat still hurt terribly, but the sound of his own voice also seemed to, well, wake him up a bit. He realized then that he'd been walking around like a zombie since last night, unable to think or plan more than a few steps at a time. Shock, probably. It wasn't a comfortable realization.

The voice of the stones cut through all his despair, loneliness and weariness. There was nothing intelligible or even comprehensible in that sound, yet it comforted him, eased his mind.

He couldn't have said when, exactly, the idea came to him. But once it occurred, certainty settled in his heart. He began to believe that he might have a choice, a purpose, a mission to fulfill. If he couldn't track Joah and Kat, he could at least find a way to their destination. He could make a way to Mere.

He surveyed his world.

To the east and south, back toward Looking Glass, the foothills crumbled to a plain that gradually became a steppe. The white spear trees spiked up from the earth like needles in the green flesh of the earth. If he turned around and started walking, he could find his way back to Blue, Rain and the rest, if he wished.

Or there was a river in those woods that might carry him even further…in any case, his past resided in the east.

The north was almost entirely obscured by a pall of smoke. The taste of sulfur was still in the air. That way was closed to him now and, perhaps, it always had been.

Dancer thought of his cryptic conversation with Henge on the caravan trail. What was Mere, exactly? He was coming to understand that it wasn't only a myth, or even a city out of Mirrorworld's forgotten history. Joah knew the truth.

All along, Dancer had worried about the wrong things. It wasn't Joah's sanity that was important, or even Kat's morality. It was Mere that he needed to understand. Joah had told him plainly several times that Mere was the key and he'd missed the obvious every time.

Dancer turned his gaze to the west where the great ragged spine of the Nabik range filled his sight, though partly curtained now by enormous clouds of smoke. From the moment he'd first seen these mountains, they had spoken to him.

He hadn't really listened. Until now.

Now, with his heart open, their voice passed into him. This range, though young for mountains, was standing when his ancestors had been out chasing mastodons. Like the Rockies back home….

When he thought of the Rockies, Dancer invariably thought of his

father and brothers—they had hiked in the mountains every weekend for as long as he could remember—but his mother had loved the mountains, too. And they'd killed her.

He'd never forgiven the mountains, but neither could he reject them. "All right, then," he croaked.

Working slowly, Dancer gathered up a few of the stones and carried them to a clear spot in the valley. He needed a guide to Mere, to the physical city, but even more to the place, the time. With a little luck, maybe he could successfully construct Joah's solar-powered telephone. He surveyed his arrangement. It was a start. If he could live long enough to finish it, he'd find his answers.

He needed to understand an essential truth and the stones were the only voice that could speak it.

As Dancer set to work on his project, illusions from the past joined him, children of his mind and memory. Sometimes, Jack squatted next to him, squinted at his brother and made some quiet comment. Brian only watched Dancer, his gaze full of worry and sorrow. His father joined him on the hunt for food. Dancer's most frequent visitor was his grandfather, who guided him with memories of a life spent as a stonemason.

His mother lived here, now. But he wasn't ready to talk to her. She was near when he caught the fish and small animals that he cleaned and cooked for his dinner, close by when he slept under stars that changed from moment to moment like a child's pinwheel, and at his side as he prepared for the journey to come.

Shades of the others appeared. Rain, Blue and the friends he'd made in Looking Glass. After a while, one or two aels even came to him. As time passed, as his creation grew, all these revenants became inhabitants of an unreal mental landscape, more real to him than he was himself, like characters in a story who have outlived their author and begun to weave their own, better, tales.

But Joah and Kat never appeared here.

◄⚬ ⚬►

Time passed, immeasurable to Dancer.

Now that he had let go of his need to track Joah and Kat, all his panic and uncertainty had gone. He took his time with every task. With the pool in the clearing continually replenished, he had abundant water, and the wildlife that had fled from the forest in the face of the fire was everywhere, so the snares he set often rewarded him with dinner. Fish in the pond were plentiful. That left him free to pursue his ultimate goal—building an instrument to summon Mere. When he found Mere, he'd find his friends.

But the tasks he set himself were often left undone or half finished as he drifted into the illusion of life that flowed around him. It was as seductive as watching a soap opera, or reliving a favorite fantasy. His own structures, as he completed them, accelerated the problem, acted as seeds from which grew a ghostly village, a half life he projected from his memories. It was difficult to remember which of the stones he saw were stones he had cut, and which were merely the idea of stones conjured by his mind.

In his saner moments, Dancer understood his danger. He was embracing madness, all on the hunch that Mere was real, that it could be called. Joah had been right. Dancer was starting to see things his way. Soon enough, the real world would be indistinguishable to him from this village of ghosts.

When he wasn't out seeking food or new stones for his project, Dancer stayed close to his crude camp and the collection of stones he had gathered from the surrounding hills. He made tools from the stone to augment the few pitiful tools in his backpack: a grinding wheel, wedges, levers of various lengths, a dozen different chisels, axes made with razor-sharp edges of chipped obsidian set into wood handles. Many times his choices failed him and he was forced to start over with a different kind of rock. But he never stopped.

It was as if he had lost any direct understanding of the passage of time. He listened to the whisper of the stones and carved a memory out of them.

One day, Dancer went to the pool for water and noticed that the fall of ash had finally ended and the surface was once again clear. He saw his own reflection in the water. His face, always a little narrow, was now hollowed out and gaunt, covered with a tangled growth of black beard. His eyes were sunken and too bright.

As he stared down at this febrile stranger, the water became still, then froze to a glassy coldness, like metal. His own visage faded away and a new vision appeared. He saw a man wearing a large pack climbing up a hill, using a polished walking stick to clear black and yellow grass from his path. The man was tall, slender, and moved with grace and determination. Dancer watched the man and it occurred to him that he had been a different person. He could no more be that man again than he could have accepted the gift—another life in an alien body—that Mere had offered on the caravan trail.

At the top of the hill, this memory of a man found a tableau of stone. The vision ended. The silver surface of the pool faded until it reflected the sky above him, and the unfamiliar man he had become.

Dancer stood up from the pool and returned to his camp. His own shrine of archways and standing stones, as near a copy of the ones he'd seen on the hill as he could manage, was nearly finished. It was the sound of the stones that had guided him. He shifted, drilled, and shaped as if the clearing was a great psychic flute and he was carving the holes that would give it voice.

Not long after the vision of the pool—a vision that haunted him now, because he felt there was some deeper truth in it that he had failed to understand—his own stone circle was finished. The sound from the stones now sang at the same pitch and timbre in his ears and mind as the one he had left behind so long ago on the hill.

At last, one morning Dancer awoke to find Henge seated cross-legged in the frame of an archway. The ael stood up, spread its deadly hands and spoke.

"We are called. We answer."

Dancer said nothing, but sent an image of the two of them traveling together. It seemed a proper symmetry. He packed his things, shouldered his pack, and followed the ael.

He didn't pause to say any goodbyes, but he did turn to look down from a height on the place he had made in these last arduous months.

The people from his mind who had populated the clearing for so long were gone. It was just a circle of roughly cut stones, empty and silent.

Henge led them into the heart of the mountains, to a trail headed by yet another of the green stone archways. Dancer stood outside the portal for some time. It was still possible to turn away. One step through that archway and the hallucinations that had plagued him from the first days he'd arrived through the Mirror would worsen.

He had a feeling that his time in the village of his own making had taught him how to live among his ghosts. But his survival was nothing. If he only cared about living, why had he followed Joah and Kat through the Mirror? The truth was, he would always be incomplete without the two of them, and he couldn't believe that they didn't feel the same way about him.

He stepped through the archway.

Henge and Dancer picked their way up the trail for the next few days. They traveled hard—moving upward through the mountains in two hour treks, then resting for an hour. Henge knew the trail very well, and the ael was also the one who found them food along the way, and shelter.

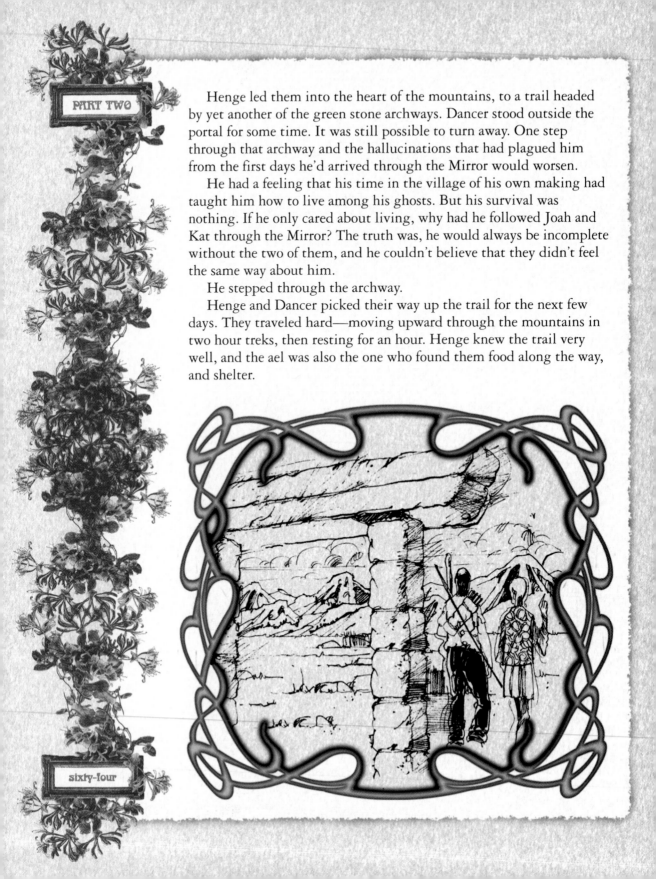

And as they traveled, they talked.

In the beginning, Dancer talked a little about his family and Earth. The ael was fascinated. In turn, Henge tried to explain what it was like to be an ael, to be a traveler in a kind of group dream of time. Neither of them really understood the other. It was only in the moment of traveling together on the Road with the caravan that the two had truly been able to communicate. But even now, with a mixture of pidgin and images, they did what they could. As they climbed upward, their friendship deepened into what, for Dancer anyway, felt like having a brother at his side.

The days flew by. Dancer's mastery of his fractured sight grew better. At times, he even dared hope that he might fuse all those shattered fragments back into one clean window into reality. It helped to talk about it with Henge, who seemed to understand perfectly what Dancer was seeing.

Dancer found himself confiding everything to Henge, his hopes, fears, and especially his guilt. It was like having a perfect therapist, one incapable of moral judgment. When he told Henge that aels could make a fortune on Mirrorworld as psychiatrists, the alien hadn't been as bewildered as he'd expected. It seemed that the sharing of memories and releasing of guilt was just as powerful a need in aels.

The journey took on a timeless beauty. Under other circumstances, Dancer could have spent a lifetime just hiking with Henge, learning about the alien's people, their history and culture and the great mystery that they called Mere. If ever they found a safe conclusion to this hunt, maybe they could do exactly that. That he, Dancer Vicksburg, was the first human being to ever truly talk to an ael was both an honor and an obligation. For awhile, he even imagined writing a book, like the codex that Pilgrim had done of the natural world, on what he had glimpsed of an alien civilization. Mere deserved a testament. Dancer knew how fortunate he was to have Henge guiding him.

One morning, the two travelers broke into a clear space with a panoramic view of the mountains, shadowed by a sky that was still tinged with gray volcanic ash. To the east, the mountain sloped down into a misty green expanse shot through with threads of red and gold. In every other direction, the blue and white mountains reached beyond sight into the sky. These mountains were sculpted by the hand of a glacier, and they seemed older and grander than anything on Mirrorworld.

Nothing on this world had reminded him so much of home. He thought of his father and brothers and their weekly climbs together in the Rockies. After his mother's death from a fall, the climbs had been

part habit, part recreation, and part memorial. He couldn't see mountains now without a spike of sadness in his heart for the woman who bore him and loved him.

By Dancer's reckoning, he and the ael had climbed about a thousand feet that day. The air was still good, not thin at all, but it was starting to get colder; their breath was visible as they panted and puffed their way up the mountain.

Henge showed his companion the route of the old path. It snaked around the western face of this mountain, then down into a hanging valley cloaked in mist. The ael hadn't spoken a word or sent any mental images on this day. Their companionship was fragile, Dancer knew that. Sometimes, it was like pretending to be asleep while actually sleeping. Dancer wondered if it wasn't his fault—he thought there was an excellent chance that Henge didn't exist at all, except in his own mind. It would make sense, then, that Henge's mood would vary as his own did. But lately, Dancer also wondered whether Joah and Kat had ever really lived, if the time they'd spent together was all a dream, if Dancer's memories of Earth were anything but a fantasy. As Dancer struggled on, the passage of time was becoming elusive to him, reality something he couldn't quite grasp, his memory as malleable as wet clay in his hands.

The path they traveled led up, always upward into the mountains. It was the one solid truth of his world. Dancer's ghosts climbed with them; he could hear them singing late at night.

◄8 8►

The path opened into a wide plateau, several hundred feet wide. There were a few structures there, made of a yellowish stone, crumbled and streaked with gray lichen. A large depression in the center of the clearing was coated with soot so old that it had become fossilized in the surrounding stone. This plateau had clearly once been a habitation of some sort—but abandoned long ago. Then, between one step forward and the next, a village appeared before Dancer's wondering eyes, exactly as it must have looked millienia ago.

The broken structures became simple stone huts whose windows and doors were covered with densely woven mats that smelled to Dancer strongly of evergreen needles. There was a stone platform built against the face of the mountain and supported by a wealth of struts. The huge fire pit was half filled with coals whose heat seeped into Dancer's bones. The waves of heat rippled the air.

Dancer took another step forward and people appeared. They were aels. But where Henge had red hair covering its body, these had sable

hair, thick and lustrous. They wore winking jewels around their waists and necks. The gems looked like uncut rubies, emeralds and sapphires. Against the midnight dark hair of the aels, they glowed like constellations of colorful stars.

The aels were roasting dinner for the village over the coals of the fire. Some very large animal had been spitted and was now being rotated by a pair of small aels whose attitude was one of great self-importance. Groups of five or more aels sat cross-legged in circles. Some of them were weaving, others repairing tears in clothes and equipment, but a few of the groups seemed to be just talking as they sat facing each other. Miniature goat-like creatures scampered everywhere, pausing occasionally to rear up like tiny stallions and paw the air with their black hooves, small as commas. When two of the little goat-things met, they'd rear up and slam their hooves together, like a pair of basketball players exchanging high fives. The aels paid them little attention.

Dancer stepped forward again and the scene became even more vivid. He heard the creak of the roasting spit as it turned and the snap of animal fat in the coals below. He smelled the meat and the sweat of a few dozen people. The crack of the goats' hooves echoed in the air. The aels did make sounds, Dancer discovered. Not speech, but squeaks from the little ones, sharp barks to each other, and underlying it all, a melodic humming, something the aels seemed especially prone to do when concentrating on a physical task.

Dancer remembered with a nearly physical pain how his mother would sing under her breath while she sewed a button or fixed a tear in a shirt. She said such tasks kept her hands busy and helped her relax after dealing with the grocery business all day. Apparently, some things transcended planetary boundaries.

A group of the smaller aels pelted from behind one of the stone huts and swirled into a big circle. The little ones made a cacophony of sounds, barks mostly. They were carrying a dirty white lumpy thing that they tossed around in high arcing throws. They were obviously playing some sort of game, and the best throws were the ones with the highest arc and the most accurate landings on some chosen target, usually an adult ael.

Dancer could hear his breath rasping in his throat and his heart beating hard and fast in his chest. *I'm losing my mind*, but he wasn't sure if he spoke aloud, or merely thought it.

Dancer glanced to his side and saw that Henge had joined him in this vision.

"Home," said the ael.

"What do you mean? Your home? My home?"

There was a rush of sound, like the wings of some vast bird. Dancer turned back to the village. It was gone. The sound of velvet thunder increased and, as a wall of snow tumbled down around him, Dancer understood in a flash. The village was destroyed in an avalanche. But was it real, or remembered? No matter. He had time only to curl into a

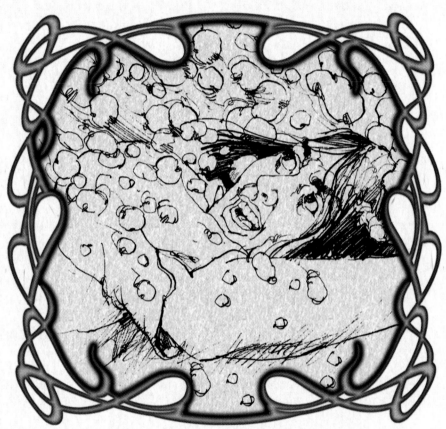

ball before he was tumbled through space in the cascading snow. He landed hard, losing the air in his lungs and his consciousness.

When he came to, Dancer was buried beneath the snow.

It was strangely warm. He couldn't move and he couldn't see. Snow surrounded him, although it was loosely packed enough that he could breathe. The snow tasted like lime on his tongue. It was such an odd discovery. On Mirrorworld, the snow tasted like lime. The realization

made him smile, an expression that felt strange on his face, unknown to the small muscles underneath his skin. When had he last smiled? Or laughed? He didn't know. Dancer closed his eyes. He could feel his ghosts around him, so close now. They were lies, really. Just lies. He was, and always would be, alone.... He felt drowsy, wondered idly if this was the last thought he'd ever have, and surrendered to sleep.

◄◊ ◊►

He was ten years old.

They were all hiking up a soft trail to a picnic spot. Jack and Brian were far ahead, but Dad and Mom kept a slower pace, pausing often to help Danny. He still hadn't got the hang of shifting his center of balance to accommodate a pack. His parents didn't seem to mind the frequent stops. They liked to look out over the valley. Dad would pull out a battered guidebook and point out the peaks by name. The Rockies were really dozens of different mountains, and each one of them had a story. Mom was quiet, just singing under her breath and smiling at her son. The hike was a short one, but it was Danny s first and he was determined to make it all the way without, as Brian put it, dumping out.

Danny's waist belt slipped a notch and his pack tilted, making the boy stumble. Dad snorted a little with suppressed laughter, and Danny felt a flush of humiliation. Mom knelt down and adjusted the strap. She looked so young in this dream. Her tanned features were softened with love, with caring. She wore a blue scarf around her red hair.

"Why don't you go ahead and see what Jackie and Brian are up to?" said his mom to Dad, quietly. "Dancer and I'll be along."

His parents exchanged looks. His dad shrugged and squeezed his youngest son's shoulder.

"Take your time. It's a fine day for walking."

After his dad left, Mom stood up and looked down into Dancer's eyes.

"He didn't mean to laugh."

"Yeah, I know."

"Why don't you break the trail, partner?"

The two of them continued up, with Dancer in the lead. The trail's slope evened out after awhile and he found the going much easier. They didn't talk as they climbed. They didn't need to.

<Nice, isn't it?>

<Yeah, Mom.>

Being able to talk like this was a special secret the two of them shared. Nobody else in the family could do it. At some point, he couldn't have said exactly when, he found the rhythm and the balance that made the pack's weight disappear into every step. It was like a magician's trick, just the way his Dad had told him it would be.

<Hey, Mom—>

<Yes, I see, Dancer. I see.>

He heard something then. Afterward, and for many years, he told himself it was Mom calling for help. He spun around and saw her fall from the side of the trail. He lunged for her, but the pack overbalanced and he fell to the ground a few inches short. Maybe he wouldn't have been strong enough to hold her up anyway.

She fell only a few dozen yards, really, but it was enough to break her neck. When his father and brothers came back to see what was delaying them, Dancer was sitting at the ledge with his thumb in his mouth and his pack thrown away.

An accident. There was never any doubt in his mind or his family's—it was an accident.

But here and now, after all these years, Dancer faced up to the truth. She hadn't called for help. She had simply called out to his mind with a single word:

<Goodbye.>

It wasn't very long before a red-haired hand reached down into the snow and pulled him out. Henge's palm was heavily callused and the claws that brushed Dancer's arm felt like bone knives.

Henge pulled him out of what should have been a soft white grave. Dancer stared up at the alien whose red hair stood out like a bloodstain against the vast whiteness around them. The ael's blue scarf whipped in the wind.

"Thanks. I guess I owe you two lives now."

The ael sent an image of Joah and Kat. Dancer felt as if the alien had sent a pair of those long, sharp nails directly into his heart. He'd known from the beginning what Henge intended, though he'd tried to pretend that he didn't. But the time for illusions was over.

Henge guided Dancer out of the blinding white nothingness. The avalanche had buried the trail completely. Dancer could see nothing but snow in every direction. But it didn't stop Henge. The ael had a pair of strangely shaped wood and leather thong plates tied to his bootsoles. Once the ael got moving, Dancer realized what the plates were for—snowshoes. Henge gestured for Dancer to follow. Dancer did his best, probing carefully with his walking stick for firm footing. It was slow and painstaking, but enough ridges of rocky outcrops were near the surface that he didn't vanish again into a snowy grave. Henge led them unerringly over the blanket of snow, up the slope, and finally to a fissure in the stone peak, where he stopped to remove his snowshoes and stow them in his pack. The snow and the mountain shielded a miracle. The gap, protected from the avalanche by an overhang of rock, led to a slit in the mountain. Taking his pack off and dragging it, turning sideways and sucking in his breath, Dancer was just able to squeeze inside after Henge. The stone scraped against his ribs and left scratches on his arms and face. They were in a cave, one small enough that Dancer had to hunch over to fit inside. Except for the glow from the slice of light at the entrance, the cavern was utterly dark. Dancer heard Henge moving inside.

"Here." The ael's voice echoed. Apparently, the ael had also decided that the time for pretense was over. No more cryptic images.

Dancer followed the sound down a slope in the ground around a curve in the wall. He used his hand against the wall as a guide and for balance. The wall felt rough and grainy in most places, like pumice or

some other porous stone, and irregular under his touch rather than smooth. Henge led them deeper into the cavern. Very soon, even the thin splinter of light from the cave's entrance was gone. In total darkness now, the two travelers descended ever deeper into the cavern. A dank mustiness suffused the air. The walls and floor of the cave—the only point of reference Dancer had in the Stygian darkness other than the sound of Henge's footsteps—were slightly damp, and Dancer occasionally stumbled through chill pools of water, praying as he did so that they wouldn't swallow him whole. Henge didn't appear to have any difficulty navigating in the darkness. In fact, the alien never hesitated, though they often moved past side passages from which gusts of icy air could be felt. How the ael knew which passage was the correct one—or if he in fact was as sure of his way as he seemed—was a mystery to Dancer.

It was difficult to judge the passage of time here, and—since the forest fire and its aftermath—Dancer didn't seem to be able to delineate discrete blocks of time. They might have walked under the earth for an hour, or many hours. Gradually, a bit of light returned, a yellowish glow from a strange bioluminescent moss in the walls. Finally, the light increased to the point that Dancer could see around him. He saw right away that these caverns had been made—carved by sentient hands. The ceiling was vaulted into a series of interlocking groins and the walls…they were beautiful. They were covered with chiseled figures. Henge had not paused, but Dancer did. He wished he had some better light, but at least the moss made it possible for him to see something of the wall writing. His fingers moved over the delicately cut symbols. He was reminded of Egyptian hieroglyphics. The ceiling of the corridor stretched many feet over his head and the symbols in the wall filled every bit of space that he could see.

Reluctantly, Dancer rushed to catch up with Henge, but he kept sneaking glances at the walls. The moss sometimes filled in the symbols in the stone so they glowed as if filled with molten gold. He wanted desperately to stop and look at them carefully. Had anyone on Mirrorworld ever seen anything like this? Maybe he was the first human ever to set eyes on this proof of an ancient civilization.

When, at last, Henge stopped, they were standing outside a massive portal that led to a sharply angled corridor, like the first turning in a stone maze. The ael turned around to face the human. Maybe it was all the time they'd traveled together, slowly forging a psychic connection, that made it possible for Henge to speak in words to Dancer. But he thought that the truth might really be found in that moment on the caravan route when he had seen white hair on his own hands.

PART TWO

seventy-three

"The end of what was is now." Henge's voice, though clearly audible, didn't echo in the enclosed space. Very strange.

Dancer studied the alien and felt a deep sadness. He had a premonition of what they would find on the other side of the portal.

"Lead on, Henge. No use in living in the past, huh?"

The ael sent an image.

<Dancer laughing.>

They stepped through the portal and Dancer instantly heard the eternal cry of the stones, which he had come to understand was the voice of Mere calling through time to any who could hear.

The corridor was an entirely different kind of stone from the rest of the cavern and he was unsurprised to see that the symbols in the wall were filled in with the green jade stuff, as well as red and blue and white stone. All of this inlay felt as smooth as pearl to the touch. The stones glowed as if a rainbow had been lovingly poured into the walls to form a bewildering variety of shapes, many of them strange to Dancer's eye. But a few were all too familiar. Among the outlines of aels, one large icon, several inches tall, was unmistakable—the curve of a green Mirror and from that Mirror an endless flow of bits of red. Dancer brought his eyes as close as he could to the tiny curves of crimson stone and nodded.

They were Bugs.

Eventually, Henge found a dry, sheltered cave where they could camp. It took a long time for Dancer to get a fire started using the moss on the walls as fuel. They shared the last bit of meat from Dancer's pack. The ael clearly didn't think much of it, but Dancer wasn't too concerned. It was better, even if not much better, than starving. He let his mind drift a bit and Joah and Kat appeared on either side of the fire. They were laughing, roasting marshmallows. Was this a memory, a wish fulfilled, or a dream? Dancer was starting to believe that there was no difference. But as he listened to their light-hearted banter, he wept for the times that were no longer, and the times that had never been.

The Children of Mere

Henge led the way out of the mass of scree and stone to the western face of the mountain. Below, buried under a gray mist, was a valley nestled in a hollow bordered on every side by the sheer face of mountains. The sun passed from early morning to noon to later afternoon as the two travelers descended a trail that often disappeared into a labyrinth of stone courses so dark that no light penetrated. Dancer felt as though the two of them were moving through the subconscious of the mountain, from light to dark to light again. Henge never faltered.

Twilight arrived, yet, amazingly, the air was still warm. The trail opened into a copse of yellow and black trees that sloped down the side of the mountain, painted now in tones of amber from the setting sun.

Finally, Henge led them to a ledge that gave a clear view though an opening in the foliage. There, framed by the gnarled trees, Dancer saw a lake of silver, surmounted by a wondrous city. It was alien—yet filled with structures that were nearly familiar. He saw bridges like spiderwebs arcing over streets that looked more like the grooves in some vast bowl of mercury than paths for channeling citizens. There were stubby fingers of some white substance, ivory or alabaster. It was hard to tell from this angle, in this uncertain light, but Dancer felt sure that these spires swirled with a paler color, like fingers of ice dripping old blood. The city was surrounded by a tall, unbroken wall as smooth as quicksilver. There was only one opening in it, gates that opened at the end of a stone path.

Dancer stared at the city of Mere for a long time. He could no longer ignore the ephemeral touch that had grown in his thoughts. Joah was in the city. So was Kat. They would surely have sensed his presence by now. He didn't even want to think about what they were doing in there—or what they were planning to do to him. Time enough for that in the morning. Dancer glanced at Henge.

"Is it real?"

"Home," said Henge.

Dancer nodded and the two companions continued their descent.

Morning came. The song of Mere was in the air and Dancer knew

that today they would enter the city, or the city would enter them. Dancer wasn't sure which was the truth, nor did he believe it mattered anymore.

He was prepared for the possibility that Joah might appear to him, or set traps in their path, but Dancer wasn't ready when Kat came instead.

Henge had gone ahead, as the ael often did, alone. Maybe the alien was hunting for food, though Dancer had never seen him do that—a taboo, perhaps?—or maybe the ael just wanted to take a crap in peace. Dancer smiled to himself. It was hard to imagine the grim, ethereal Henge doing anything so mundane.

"You shouldn't have come, Dancer."

There, a few steps down the trail, stood Katmandu Fury. She wore a plain, white gown that set off the bronze glow of her skin. Her features were delicate, but strong, as if she were a brass sculpture formed by a master artist. Kat's hair, black and straight, had been recently cut close to her skull. Her hands were clasped in front of her. Dancer liked her hands, veined and capable.

"Hi, Kat." His voice sounded so old in his ears. "Looks like you and Joah are trying to start a new hair fashion trend."

An unwilling smile twitched her lips.

"I like the beard."

Dancer self-consciously touched the brambles on his face.

She turned around and began to walk. Dancer followed. For all he knew, Kat might be leading him to his death.

Soon, the two of them were walking side by side through the broadleaf trees that smelled so much like evergreens to Dancer. Mere was no longer visible. As they walked, they talked.

"Why now, Kat? I've been calling to you for months."

"Do you really want to know?"

He looked sidelong at her, at the combination of grace and serenity he could sense from her, even in this psychic sending. Some deep joy filled her. He had never been jealous of Joah, really, though of course he'd known that the two of them were lovers. He'd never felt excluded from their love. Until now. Was this the real reason he'd chased them through the Mirror? Was it all that simple?

"Yes," he said. "I need to know."

She opened a door in her thoughts for him and he felt the touch of a new small mind groping blindly, weakly.

"You're pregnant?"

She nodded.

"We knew I couldn't hide that from you if we ever linked."

Dancer felt such a storm of feelings that, for a time, he couldn't think coherently. One thing stood out clearly, though—the wreckage of the Gray Quarter in Looking Glass, where many had died, even children. He couldn't hide that thought from Kat, and her reaction was full of confusion and pain and regret.

"I warned as many as I could," she said.

But both of them knew how empty that sounded. He didn't like hearing the weakness in her voice. He'd never known Kat to hide from consequences. For a while, they walked on in silence. Then Dancer spoke.

"Why is he letting you talk to me?"

For the first time, Kat showed a flash of temper.

"Joah doesn't own me, Dancer. I'm here because I want to be. Whatever you think, this place *is* the answer to the Bugs."

"All right," he replied, mildly. "Then why haven't you spoken to me sooner?"

She wouldn't answer.

"Should I guess? I think maybe you both knew that I'd never give up as long as I thought I was chasing you."

"What do you mean?"

The two of them broke out of the foliage and into a clearing. The way to Mere was clear. He turned to her and smiled.

"You and Joah have been here all along. *You've* been chasing *me.*"

Her expression didn't change.

"I told him you wouldn't be fooled."

"But how? Why? And why did you send an ael to lead me here?"

Kat frowned. "An ael? What are you talking about?"

Dancer looked behind Kat to see Henge standing there, blue head scarf riffling in the wind. The ael had found a length of wood to use as a walking stick. Dancer pointed at Henge and Kat turned, but saw nothing, or else pretended that she saw nothing. Dancer felt chilled. In either case, he was faced with a terrifying truth.

"Why did you lure me here, Kat?"

She faced him and her face split into the old sweet smile that he loved.

"We need you, Dancer. We've always needed you, but after Looking Glass, we thought you wouldn't come."

He tried to smile. Hadn't those been the words he'd prayed to hear?

"Well, I guess I'll see you soon then."

She raised a hand and went away.

Henge stared at him.

"Yeah," he said, softly. "I know. She lied."

Henge handed him the walking stick and closed a callused hand briefly over his own. The ael smelled of musk. His clothes, the vest and kilt, showed signs of hard wear and travel. The blue head scarf danced in the wind. The ael was real, as real as Dancer himself.

Did I ever actually leave the village of ghosts? he wondered. *Am I still there now, dreaming this journey's end?*

"Here, now, the end of the beginning," said Henge.

Dancer looked at the being who he'd come to think of as a friend. Was Henge a ghost? *Worse,* he wondered, *am I a ghost, some memory of Joah's conjured out of madness and regret?*

There was only one way to answer that question.

"Let's see," he said.

◀᳁ ᳁▶

The closer they came to the gates of Mere, the more clearly Dancer saw that the city was an empty shell. The pink streaks he had seen on the misshapen towers were flowering vines that covered vast areas of Mere. The pink and red flowers gave off a scent like roses, but with a bitter undertone.

The gates hung in three parts, cunningly fitted together with mortise and tenon hinges, the same sort of masonry he'd seen at work in the tori archways of the shrine he'd seen on the hill so long ago. The surface of the gates was covered with more of the symbols and hieroglyphs. It would take days to study them all. The sun's rays showed one section of the city with a mirror and a cloud of red curves arcing out of it. The Bugs had been here.

Through the gates, a massive fountain stood, chipped and scarred by the ages. Those ubiquitous gray vines snaked over it. Beyond the fountain were asymmetrical towers of alabaster, also cloaked in gray vines and pink flowers. Cobbled streets wove away into the city in every direction.

Henge strode purposefully down one of the streets opposite the fountain. Dancer paused to look inside the enormous scalloped bowl of cracked stone. It was filled with the yellow bones of birds and small animals.

Dancer didn't have much of an understanding of architecture, but he thought that the structures of Mere were a strange conglomeration. At one moment, the street would narrow and massive granite walls loomed out in blocky profusion. Turn a corner and the buildings were set apart and cut from silky blocks of pastel colored marble. Another turning and everything was curves and arches, filigreed and gothic.

No matter what style of construction he saw, however, everything gave a sense of oppressive age and emptiness. The clatter of their walking sticks against the stone of the streets was the only sound they heard. Even the birds, insects, and animals Dancer would have expected in a city long vacant were absent. The deeper Henge led him into the city, the more signs of destruction Dancer saw. He wondered if the cracked and tumbled masonry surrounding him had been brought down by that earthquake he'd felt so many miles away, or by something older, and possibly much worse.

Henge paused only once during their travels. The alien stood before a door that had been carved to look like an eye, with the heavy lidded look so distinctive of an ael. Henge ran one claw lightly over the surface. When Dancer caught up to the ael, he asked what the significance of the door was, but Henge did not seem to wish to reply, a trait that Dancer was starting to understand was part of the ael's personality, rather than a sign that he didn't know how to communicate in Dancer's language.

From the moment that they had entered Mere, Dancer had been unable to locate either Joah or Kat. The internal hum of Mere itself drowned out all other psychic signatures. However, as Henge led them deeper into the heart of the city, a different mental sound did become detectable. It was an odd sound and Dancer found it hard to describe. It was partly a high whistle, not so urgent as a teakettle steaming, but as piercing somehow. It also reminded him of a clarinet note held forever, but meant for a conclusion. He couldn't say what he felt about it. It wasn't quite annoying, nor was it at all restful. Arresting, maybe.

Henge was definitely bringing them to it. It occurred to Dancer that Henge must be more closely attuned to these sorts of sounds. Or… what if it was the other way around? What if these sounds were an answer to the presence of Henge?

Sooner than he expected, they passed out of the labyrinth of the city and into a circular space many hundreds of yards in diameter. It was a flat glassy space empty of all but one thing, the source of the discordant noise and the answer to at least part of the mystery of Mere.

There, in the center of this place stood a Mirror, dead black and as tall as a skyscraper from Earth. Dancer stared at the huge thing, craning his neck to take it all in. He had never seen a Mirror so large, nor one whose surface was black. He joined Henge, who stood before the thing like an acolyte before an altar. The Mirror's call was clear now. Dancer could nearly understand its message, but not quite, as if it were whispering in a language that he had once known. Henge turned to Dancer and the ael's dark slitted eyes seemed to judge him.

"Here, now, the beginning of the end," said Henge, and without another word he walked into the blackness of the Mirror and disappeared as if he had never been.

Dancer blinked and took a step closer to the thing. He reached out a tentative hand, but didn't quite dare to touch the surface of the Mirror.

<Dancer!>

If not for Kat's mental shout, Joah's attack would have caught him completely by surprise. Dancer fell back as Joah ran forward with a length of what looked like blue pipe. Though he moved enough to avoid the worst of the blow, it was enough to knock the breath out of Dancer's lungs and send him stumbling to one knee. Joah didn't hesitate, but swung again. Dancer whipped up his walking stick with one hand and slapped Joah's blow aside.

Dancer stood up and skipped back a few steps while he recovered his breath. He didn't want to kill this man that he'd come so far to find and talk to. Joah, whatever he'd become, had once been his best friend. Dancer couldn't just kill him, could he? But Joah wasn't operating on the same set of rules. Anyone but a biotrooper would have been incapacitated by that first blow. Joah circled Dancer. His eyes burned in his face like reflections of the sun.

"Joah—"

In reply, Joah took a sliding step forward and swung a vicious swing at Dancer's head. Dancer blocked the blow with his stick. The wood rang in his hands and chips flew. A splinter slashed a gash below Dancer's right eye. Whatever Joah was using to attack him, it was

heavier and tougher than wood, and Joah was using every bit of his considerable strength to swing it.

For the next several moments, however, Dancer didn't have the time or breath to do anything but answer an unrelenting series of attacks from Joah. He was running out of options. Every furious blow he deflected further weakened Dancer's own weapon. He dreaded the moment when it would crack in his hands. A quick glance around didn't offer any obvious substitutes. If and when his walking stick fractured for that last time, he'd be defenseless against Joah's attacks. Could Dancer mount an attack of his own? Was he willing to do what it would take to survive—fight to kill? Joah paused, frowned, and Dancer sensed that he was in contact with Kat.

Joah had tried to kill him like this before, in psychic attacks, but Kat had always been able to deflect him, calm him down. But this time…something felt different. Joah was too focused, too enraged to be stopped.

Dancer's one-time best friend overcame whatever momentary distraction he'd been struggling with. He dropped his blue pipe and reached inside his coat to bring out a loaded slingshot. Kat was the real expert with the sling, but at this distance, a dozen feet, the slingshot would be as deadly as a .22. Joah's thin lips were curved in a cruel smile. Would he really use it? Could Joah kill him? Dancer didn't wait to find out. He spun on his heel and leapt into the dead Mirror.

❀ ❀

Dancer stood at the top of the hill where he had first seen the Stonehenge-like circle of shrines. He turned completely around, but the Mirror was gone. Mere had vanished. His clothes were still covered in that rancid butter stuff and his pack, unscorched, lay propped against one of the standing stones. He felt completely different, rested and strong. Dancer stroked his bare cheeks and chin. His beard was gone. His body was fit, healthy—no burn scars from the fire, and he had lost the emaciated look he'd acquired during the weeks he'd spent building a stone circle and a mental village in the foothills of the Nabik mountains. His mind was whole again, unscarred by Joah's madness.

"What's happening to me?"

He could remember everything that had occurred to him, the wedding guests in the canoe, the earthquake and volcano—but the sky was clear blue, with no sign of ash—the avalanche, the journey under the mountain…he remembered everything. It must have happened.

Dancer closed his eyes, tried to calm down. A sense of terrible panic was overwhelming him. He needed to relax, try to think about what had just happened. What day was it? Had the dark Mirror of Mere sent him back in time, somehow? If so, where was Henge? Dancer let his mind reach out and discovered that he could no longer feel anything psychically. He was deaf to the song of the shrine and he couldn't sense Joah and Kat at all. It was as if he had forgotten something obvious and long-known, like whistling. His mental ability was gone completely. He wasn't sure how he felt about that yet.

He wandered among the stones of the shrine, putting his face right up against the jade chip designs. He concentrated as tightly as he could, but he heard nothing, no hint of any psychic call.

Finally, he sat down on the hilltop next to his pack and propped his chin in his hands. He had to face the other possibility, that nothing he had experienced had really happened. Since leaving Looking Glass, Dancer had felt increasingly disconnected from things. He had suffered frequent hallucinations. It was possible, he supposed, that he had imagined the sound of the shrine, Henge, their journey—although he couldn't as yet believe that emotionally. *But why couldn't he sense his triptych?* Dancer frowned. *Could the mental battles with Joah have been hallucinations? Was that possible?* Dancer shoved back the right sleeve of his jacket and woolen tunic. His forearm was smooth and unscarred. Dancer kept flexing that mental muscle that had been available to him since childhood, to no effect.

What if…what if he'd never really been connected to Joah and Kat telepathically? Or, rather, what if Joah had somehow tricked him into believing he was telepathically bound to him and Kat from the beginning, on Earth?

But that was impossible, wasn't it? What should he do? His goal for so long—to find Joah and Kat, and try to reason with them—was suddenly out of reach when he'd come so close, so close…. Dancer felt so confused and lost. In the village of ghosts, he had learned the difference between memory and time, but now that elusive sense of the fluidity of reality escaped him.

Dancer ran his fingers through his hair. A light breeze had sprung up and he smelled a tang in the air that he recognized as the herald of rain. He stood uncertainly. To the west, lay that fabulous sweep of forest and the Nabik range beyond that. The spine of mountains was little more than a hazy outline in the distance. Should he retrace his steps, or…if he hadn't really made that journey…what was the use of going that way? Dancer looked to the east, back the way he'd come. A day's walk would bring him back to the farming community he'd stayed at…and another week's hike should bring him to Danvi where he could hitch a ride to Looking Glass….

Intermittent drops of light rain splashed against his face. Dancer swung his pack over one shoulder and scurried under the lintel arch of one of the shrines. It wasn't much protection, but enough that he had time to unpack the roll of oilcloth that he used to insulate his sleeping roll and drape it over his head and pack.

The rain began to fall more heavily and the sky turned gray, as if only belatedly realizing that it was full of rain and bound to pour it somewhere. Dancer hunched under his makeshift shelter in a state of dazed confusion. There, under the lintel of what he persisted in regarding as one of the children of Mere, he tried to make some sense of the enigma he was wrapped in. He just couldn't get a handle on things. It was inconceivable to him that all he had learned and suffered in his journey to Mere was only a dream. Yet, here he was, sitting in a rapidly expanding puddle of muddy water, and no effort of will he could muster produced any psychic response.

He could go back to Looking Glass. The idea was growing in Dancer's mind. It held the same sort of attraction and hope as the moment when the wedding guests in the canoe had mysteriously made a place for him in their midst. It was the peace of making a choice for the known. He wanted that, to know, to be at rest.

Still, there was Henge. Dancer realized that he'd been so preoccupied with his hunt for Kat and Joah that he'd never really stopped and thought carefully about the ael and what they'd shared. The alien had saved his life at least twice, guided him in places that he would never have found on his own, and been a source of frequent confusion. But maybe that was only because Dancer hadn't seriously listened to the ael and thought about what he'd said.

He cast his mind back over the conversations they'd had. Surely, these were memories, not hallucinations?

"Here and now," Dancer murmured, trying the words out loud.

Henge had repeated the phrase more than once and the ael was not the sort of person who spoke idly. It was funny, in a way. Henge was a complete mystery to him in so many ways, an alien. He didn't even know if the ael was male, female, or something entirely different. Yet, the ael had become a friend, with identifiable quirks and a personality.

"Here and now," Dancer repeated to himself.

He understood the ael's meaning well enough. In the village of the ghosts, Dancer had learned to live outside of time, to accept memory as disconnected from sequence and intent.

That's fine, but how can you live like that? If you want to survive, you have to plan. You've got to use the past to prepare for the future, so—

And then he had it. Wasn't that precisely what Mere had done? It was a city out of time, with a tragic past and a weapon that must inevitably endanger the future, as if the Mirror were a loaded gun left lying out for anyone to pick up, for Joah to pick up, and fire into the present.

What if the people of Mere found a way to hide their dangerous city in time? But not time as a human might understand it, not a raft on a river flowing from then to perhaps, but another sort of place, the universe of memory. Then Joah Cray arrives on Mirrorworld. Joah Cray, whose mind is broken in a most unusual way. He is obsessed with the Bugs, unbreakably determined to find them. His fabulous psychic gifts, augmented by Kat, opened a way to Mere. But once there...what? Dancer shook his head, coming out of his reverie. The rain had slackened and the sky was opening up. He saw a double rainbow with the colors all in shades of red and blue. Rainbows...the sight tickled his memory, but a clear thought wouldn't coalesce.

He stood up and shook out his oilcloth, snapping away the moisture. Dancer smiled slightly. He could spin all the philosophical fantasies he wanted to about memory and time and magic cities, but he was just a man alone in the wilderness, hungry, tired, and now soaked through from a very real rainstorm.

How do you let go of then and perhaps and live only in the here and now and still get anything done?

He could just about see the look on his father's face if he'd asked that plain-spoken man such an airy question. Suddenly, he missed his family fiercely. Jack, with his affected drawl and sly wit. Brian, the worrier who hid his concern in sarcasm. Dad, who had learned how to live a life alone. Dancer looked up at the sky and felt a certain grim certainty settle in him. Mere was real. The journey he remembered had happened.

And along the way, he'd finally faced the truth about his mother. Maybe some of his reluctance to accept the truth of Mere was his inability to accept that old guilt.

Then there was Kat. Did he really want to deny what he knew was true? If he did, wasn't he exhibiting the same sort of cowardice that had led her to hurt all those people in the Gray Quarter? Like it or not, Dancer Vicksburg wasn't going to hide from the truth. His family hadn't raised him that way.

"All right then," he said, his voice sounding almost confident in his own ears. "The question isn't so much how *I* can live in the here and now, but how Joah manages it. He's got to have some reason for the mind games he's been playing with me, some plan. If he isn't completely nuts."

But of course, he's living in the timeless, mutable reality of Mere, too. He and Kat. Dancer frowned. *Wait a minute, though. Is Kat really there with him? Or, a better question, when is she with him?* But no. He was making the same mistake again. *Mere isn't lost in time, but memory. Whose memory?* Dancer's mouth dropped open and he gave a short amazed laugh. *Who else?*

Henge.

And where in all the vast mountains of memory would Dancer most surely find the ael? Beside the river? In the village of ghosts? Down in the dark of the Nabik caverns? Or...Dancer smiled to himself. Or at the source of the rainbow, the hint that Henge had given to him more than once.

Dancer settled down in the archway of one of the trilithon archways. He sat cross-legged, closed his eyes and let his mind drift into memory, to the place where he had first crossed the path of a fellow traveler. He knew what shape to wear.

◄8 8►

Was it dawn's light, or twilight? Sunset or sunrise? Mirrors of expectation. The human in the sleeping bag jerked up and stared with a mixture of astonishment and fear at Dancer-Henge. He had to ease that fear, give the man a clue to the truth, but only a clue. There is another traveler with the gift of sculpting memory. Dancer-Henge saw him. In the human's current, limited sight, the other man was bald and roughly clothed. To Dancer-Henge, Joah Cray is in constant fluid change, every movement a stroboscopic amalgam of the idea of movement.

The two men faced one another. Joah's expression changed into a multitude of faces, but Dancer-Henge was getting the knack of focusing on the essence; intention is the key to the core of memory. Joah is already centered. It is a paradox. This man who is so terribly lost in so many ways is completely at home in this chaos. It was the fractured window of memory that Joah had lived with and mastered all of his life. It was a perfect metaphor for the possibilities available to a being who has joined with Mere and entered the city's Now, the river of time and memory composed of all the thinking beings who had ever lived in the city.

There are levels of memory, Dancer-Henge thought. *I've found one of the circles, but it's not enough. I'm…we're going to have to figure out how to enter Joah's memory, his connection to Mere.* The idea that he would have to find a way into the maelstrom of Joah Cray's madness again frightened Dancer. All along, Joah had tried to tell him that madness was Dancer's destiny. It was apparent Joah was right.

◄❧ ❧►

Time and space puzzled him now. In fact, it was hard for him to think chronologically, to discipline his movements to match those of the human, but he found, with practice, that it could be done. Dancer-Henge confronted a different set of problems not as easily mastered.

He had entered the memory of Mere, or at least the memory of an ael, Henge, left behind as a guardian. Henge had lived a long and varied life on Mirrorworld before he was called to the timeless city, to become a special part of its tapestry of Now. As Dancer-Henge entered the forest, memories of the ael's lifetime whirled around. He was a child, not yet Touched and for now, he lived in the animal world. A thousand Henges—for the name given by Dancer was the only one the ael had ever known, a gift more precious than the human could ever imagine, at least until he found the Now—played in the sky with the ruu, what Dancer would have called the chimp-koalas. There were so many of that child. Some of Henge's endless sorrow eased to see that timeless joy again filtered through the human's own understanding of childhood. Who would have guessed that aels and humans could be so much the same?

But there were a thousand, a thousand times a thousand, less pleasant memories here and one that was both dangerous and necessary. Henge allowed the wedding to become marginally more real. Oh, the terrible ache of this memory! He was only a guardian, sent to the north corner, to ward for his dearest friend, who would mate with their mutual love. Momentarily, Dancer was confused by the blurring of sexes and the strange indescribable conjoining that marriage implied for an ael. But Dancer-Henge had no difficulty understanding the pain of knowing that the one you love has chosen the other one you love. A-a-a-i-i a-e-o-o-o...the song of binding rumbles easily from his chest. The oar is warm in his hands. The two whom he loves are already almost gone from the ael-Now, building a timebound marriage. They are lost to him. Was he ever a part of them? Again, Henge cries out the warding song, and in his secret heart sings a threnody. Let them be joined! There will be children, then more souls in the Now. It is the way of the ael, older even than Mere. But is also a kind of death.

The human has also released the moment of need and resumed his trek. Dancer-Henge remains in the forest. He is still learning how to resonate with this incarnation of Dancer. It's so hard to move. It seems as if all of memory ought to be accessible anywhere, but he is not that proficient, yet. Joah, on the other hand, has already found the lord of memory, the city of Mere. What is his intention? Joah has set so many of these dominoes in motion. The Henge part of Dancer believes that the man is only mad, but the human knows better. Joah is broken, insane with a rage that sings to the buzzing of bees, but not without purpose.

On the plain, Henge witnesses the lovemaking of two humans. It is a powerful locus. Kat and Joah, in the moment of intercourse, are merged, absolute inhabitants of the Greater Now, that mystery that not even Henge fully comprehends. He watches the two, though it is with an ache of both loss and separation. But he can't turn away. The child is formed and, ah, what a wonder. Here is a new soul born to the Now. Here is the instrument of the music of memory. Henge can touch the being's essence with ease and it is a balm to his heart. The ael is soothed by a reminder of the mystery of the Now, while the man is glad of a new pure life. Again, the two are merged, like lines on a graph who have met at the origin. He is Dancer-Henge again, a marriage of purpose that is increasingly becoming as natural as life to both of them.

Now the man arrives at the site of the fire and uses the sacred wood. It is a dual trap, Dancer-Henge realizes. For it drives the timebound human into an unprepared Now, while snagging Henge into the human's limitations. He should be studying this milieu.

It is in the Here and Now that he will defeat Joah, if such a thing is possible. Every detour into Then and Perhaps is a distraction and a snare.

Dancer-Henge follows Then-Dancer. It is something like looking through a window into a place of great beauty, yet continually refocusing the eye to see the composition of the window's glass. The Now draws him. How can anyone not see and understand it?

They are in the forest and now a moment of great danger and opportunity has come. For Then-Dancer, the caravan trail ahead is only a path through a physical reality. But to Dancer-Henge, this is the great Road to Mere, a moebius strip of memory that is so old it dwarfs his comprehension. All the aels who have ever made the journey to Mere have traveled this Road. It is possible for Dancer-Henge to be caught here, swept into a Now so immense and necessary that his connection to the human Then-Dancer will be forever lost. But it is also a chance to communicate clearly for the first time. The Now is everywhere, here. This is the moment to teach Dancer what he will need to know to build the village, to begin the journey.

But he has forgotten Joah, a more accomplished master of the possible. Dancer-Henge has only begun to speak to Dancer, to offer the first lesson in memory, when Joah appears in the caravan flow. He is dressed in an ael's flesh, but Dancer-Henge knows the knot of the man's soul. Joah sees, understands. He can't divorce Henge from Dancer—that is beyond anyone's power—but he can drive Then-Dancer deeper into the memory of Mere, where Then-Dancer will be lost. There is only one solution, to break the connection and send Then-Dancer to a moment on the Road which not even Joah can manipulate. Then-Dancer, only now glimpsing a piece of the puzzle, is drawn to a different frame, the eruption of Taii.

Again, the explosion, fire, gray blindness, terror. Traveling in the Now is no shield from pain and fear. Dancer-Henge loses track of Dancer and they are sundered. But it's much worse than that. Dancer-Henge is trapped among the eternally dead on the Road in a world that is now smoke and ash. He is overwhelmed with grief at the sight of so many souls lost, the diminishment of the Road, the end of his people. He cries out to Joah, as he would to a fellow ael, to witness, to share their grief. Joah seems to understand. He is, in many ways, closer to understanding the heart of an ael then even Then-Dancer.

"My condolences," said Joah.

There he is, still a blur of possibilities. He has chosen a manifestation of regret. Dancer-Henge's heart grieves at the realization that Joah Cray is most familiar with the memories of regret.

He sends Joah an image of Kat and the man nods. The image is of Kat leading Dancer to safety.

"Yes," said Joah, but it was an answer to a different question. If he could understand what that question was, he would understand all of Joah's intent.

The two men stood in a rain of ash and fire. The ruu were dying. Fragile little children of a gentler Now, they were unable to escape. In a way, Joah was responsible, just as he owed the debt for the dead of Looking Glass. He sent the man an image. Joah's golden eyes were quiet now. The feverish light was dimmed. They were alone at a moment when even the great memory of Mere was doubtful.

Dancer-Henge showed Joah the graves in Looking Glass and Joah didn't turn aside. Whatever else could be said of Joah Cray, he had never been afraid to face a hard truth.

"This is war, my friend."

But the words were wistful and his expression reminded him of that younger Joah, before the operations on his mind changed something crucial. He had been a man of honor and hope and in the eye of memory, there was no escape from the pitiless gaze of truth. Perhaps the fragmentation of Joah's mind could have been healed, in time.

"Go then," said Joah and opened a different sphere of the Now for his enemy, his friend.

The village of ghosts was a child's fumbling attempt at building a bridge to the Now. The inhabitants were shadows, puppets marched through a tattered mind's delusion of memory. He watched Dancer at work as if watching a talented, but foolish, child deliberately avoiding every hard choice. Dancer refused to really *see* his mother. Delusion is the enemy of true memory. Dancer-Henge couldn't enter the Now until he accepted his own Then, without the lies. Every lie deforms the Now. Joah might be a sad and dangerous soul now, but he never flinched from his own complicities.

As Dancer-Henge watched Then-Dancer try to build something out of the wreck of his soul, he understood something else. Joah wanted him to guide Dancer, to bring him to Mere. The attack, that seemingly mortal threat, had all been to drive Dancer into the memory of Mere. But why? If Joah and Kat were there, in Mere, didn't they have what they'd sought, a means to follow the Bugs through the Mirror? Isn't that what they wanted? Certainly, it was what Joah wanted. Why did they need Dancer?

The village of ghosts grew, like a diorama built from imperfectly

imagined hopes. Much of what Dancer made was dream, not memory, the Now adulterated with Perhaps. That was always the danger of trying to carve something out of memory. Dancer-Henge's own people knew the seduction very well. Why else would they marry and surrender eternity? Dancer-Henge sighed with the old grief. Losing a love was an infinite loss. How had these aels learned to accept it? How did the heart heal when the memories not only didn't fade, but couldn't?

Dancer-Henge saw that Dancer was at the edge of sanity, driven to a grief of madness by his encounter with the storm of pain at the center of Joah's mind. The man was scrawny, his face lost in a black tangle of beard and the eyes were sunk deep in his face, seeing nothing, and too much, fractured in many jagged windows. Here. Now. The next passage. The labyrinth under Taii, which the aels named the Mountain of Thought.

◄8 8►

The two of them stood on the ledge, which Dancer-Henge now knew by its old name: Ta-Mere, the Threshold. They were approaching a conclusion and Dancer-Henge was no closer to understanding Joah's design.

The Now flowed to the moment of Kat's appearance. Dancer-Henge looked at her through the eyes of memory as she spoke to Dancer. Dancer-Henge could see her in an entirely different aspect. Her spirit lived almost entirely in the Perhaps, drawn there by the child. When she turned to face him, Dancer-Henge knew she could see him and that she knew who he was. The faint echo of Then glowed around her, the girl who dreamed the death of her family at a picnic and believed the dream made it so, the woman who made guilt into an enemy, the biotrooper taught an ethic of duty married to the need for vengeance. The woman who loved a man deeply broken inside.

They were nearing the convergence of memories. Soon, all Nows must merge. The sight of Kat, pregnant with the essence of hope, gave Dancer-Henge a clue, because he knew that Joah had intended for Then-Dancer to know about the child. In a flash of understanding, Dancer-Henge saw at least a part of the tapestry. Joah was manipulating Kat, too, maneuvering her like a chess piece into Then-Dancer's path.

It was time for them to enter the city, or let the city enter them.

◄8 8►

Dancer-Henge stood transfixed, heart filled with surprise and old joy. Mere glowed before them, but not the sad and broken shadow that Then-Dancer saw. Dancer-Henge saw the true Mere, the city that lived in the Now and the Greater Now. Every stone, every atom of every stone, was energized with the meditations and clean thought of the people of Mere who had traveled here for millennia. It was here that the aels who had mastered the purity of Now came to add their small clarity to a creation that had been built when the Nabik mountains were yet a possibility of the Perhaps. Mere was the moment of harmony, a song that echoed forever in time.

Mere glimmered under the weight of an infinity of rainbows. They were the great weakness of aels, those dances of light caught in the lens of rain. Rainbows were remembered and woven into the Now of Mere. Every rainbow ever remembered. Dancer-Henge walked into the city and for some time forgot who he was, when, why. Rainbows.

Finally, he recalled a little of the old Now, but already Dancer was disappearing into a Then that didn't matter. He glanced in the fountain, which had sustained countless tiny lives forever. It was filled with life, birds singing out the Now, animals dancing, fish swimming, the smallest children of Mere. Dancer-Henge led his Then-brother into the heart of the city.

What Then-Dancer had seen as an amalgam of architectural styles, Dancer-Henge experienced at the moment of creation and the conclusion. To the aels, it was not the utility of the structure that mattered, but the work of time. To build with grace was more important than the creation itself.

He paused at a door and reached toward it, a sweet sorrow filling his heart. Born behind that door was the child of one whom he had loved and the love, too, was born there. It was only a little story, a tiny piece of memory of Dancer-Henge's own humble Now, but how he wished he could show it to Then-Dancer, who so grieved for a lost love.

On they went, and as they moved deeper into the heart of the city, the Nows began to merge. Dancer-Henge was losing his capacity to understand the Then of his friend, the one who had named him, who had, in a way, created him. Just as Then-Dancer on the caravan Road, Dancer-Henge was in danger of disappearing into that ancient resonance of souls.

The Mirror.

At last, Dancer-Henge understood and let out a cry of loss and rage, and guilt.

It was Joah who brought the Mirror to Mere, his memory making the portal a part of the Greater Now and, surely, it would open and spew forth apocalypse, must already have done so. Joah brought the fruit of death into the Garden. Dancer-Henge couldn't sort out the linear possibilities, or even interact with them. Only Then-Dancer could do that. He turned to the man, mind speaking to mind, willing the human to understand.

"Here, now, the beginning of the end."
He leapt into the Mirror.

◄8 8►

Dancer turned away from the Mirror and faced Joah, who lowered his weapon. All the memories of Dancer-Henge were with him. Now, at last, he was attuned to Mere. Joah studied Dancer for a long moment.

"Good," he said. Joah walked up to Dancer and clasped the taller man's forearms in a powerful grip. "Good. Now you're ready."

But Dancer was still struggling for his mental balance. So many things to consider. But one thing was clear. He broke Joah's grip and slammed the side of his fist into the smaller man's throat. Joah stumbled backwards, eyes wide with shock and pain. The buzzing of bees was very loud now. How many times had Joah's father beaten his mother into a similar look?

Dancer felt as if something precious inside of him had shattered. But he couldn't take the chance of Joah recovering. He lunged forward, striking him again and again, each blow serious and deadly. Finally, he snapped a kick with his powerful leg to the other man's kidney. The blow sent Joah to one knee. Joah's mouth worked, but no sound came. Clearly, he was desperate to speak, but what could the man say? There was no excuse, no explanation for what he'd done. Joah had brought the very evil he hated to Mere and thus to Mirrorworld itself. Dancer's eyes stung, but he couldn't afford the luxury of pity, or compassion now. He could think of no other answer. Joah had to die to destroy the Mirror.

"Dancer, no!"

It was Kat. She stood there, with her hands raised and a bit of breeze ruffled the white gown she wore. In that moment, he loved her so much.

"He made the Mirror."

"I know, but—"

"But you love him and he's the father of your child."

She looked completely dumbfounded and he felt his heart break for a second time. He could almost understand the terrible purpose that had driven her to conspire with Joah in the bombing of the library in Looking Glass. For a way to destroy the Bugs, she would do anything. But to discover that she would surrender that purpose for her own happiness and need…maybe he'd never really known her at all. He could forgive Joah more easily.

"You don't understand—"

But he did, all too well. And he knew what he should do. Even so, he hesitated. But what Joah had done would be the end of all of them,

Kat and her baby included. Surely she must see that? He opened his mouth to say this and saw that she had drawn back her own sling.

"You can't kill him, Dancer, because—"

But he didn't want to hear her betray everything she'd ever believed in. For a third time, he escaped into the Mirror of Mere.

◄⑧ ⑧►

This time, Dancer didn't return to the fateful hilltop. He didn't return to Mirrorworld at all. The Mirror sent him to a hiking path in the Rockies, into the memory that he had not yet truly faced.

<Yes, I see, Dancer. I see.>

He turned around to smile at his mother and saw that beloved face snarled in pain and tears.

<Mommy?>

<I'm sorry, my little Dancer, my joy.>

Because they were touching mind to mind and she opened her deepest thoughts to him, he saw and understood everything, the pain and despair and terror. She was dying. Everyone knew, Jack, Brian and Daddy, everyone. She was dying and this might be her last hike. She was dying.

<NO!>

But it was true and she was so afraid. But there was something else Dancer needed to know and understand.

<NO! You can't leave me like this!>

And he ran to her, but the pack slipped again and he stumbled and he fell against her, oh, just a little, just enough. He'd wanted to hit her, or hug her, but…she lost her footing, fell back.

She fell back and down and had time for only one last thought.

<Goodbye.>

And here, now, Dancer was able to hear that last thought entirely for the first time, so full of love and no trace of fear.

◄⑧ ⑧►

They were walking around a lake, he and Kat. For once, Joah wasn't with them. He was in surgery, as a matter of fact, receiving the first of the Triptych treatments that would change everything. In a short time, he would return to them with eyes that burned.

For now, though, Dancer and Kat walked together under a starry moonless sky. He'd known from the first that Kat and Joah were meant for one another. The two of them would push every limit of the biotrooper enhancements, dare any risk, to find and destroy the Bugs. The two of them were True Believers, and Dancer often wondered why he and Kat were such close friends, because he had no intention of taking a one-way trip on a dubious mission of vengeance. He'd never hated the Bugs, not like Joah and Kat.

"Penny for your thoughts, Dancer," said Kat.

She was wearing her white dress uniform and her velvet black hair was twined into a French braid. She brushed tendrils of her hair out of her eyes and Dancer was mesmerized by the grace of those strong hands.

"The truth?" he said, softly. "I was just thinking how beautiful you are, how lucky I am to know you."

She smiled, the little half grin she gave him when she thought he was being silly, but the smile faded as she looked into his eyes. Bleakness descended.

"You're not going to try and talk me into staying, I hope?"

Dancer shook his head and buried his hands in his pockets, no longer able to look directly at her.

"Nah. I know better than that." He glanced sidelong at her with a sad smile. "But I guess you're going to keep trying to talk me into going through."

Kat paused to rest a hand on his shoulder and he stopped, too. She stood up on her toes and kissed him lightly on the lips.

"We love you, Dancer."

He nodded, but swallowed back a reply. Better not to say anything now. Pretty soon, Kat and Joah would be accelerated, maybe end up commanding a strike team. Dancer would stay behind, do his mandatory two years and move on.

"We need you."

Dancer whipped his gaze to Kat to see that she had entered the memory in her Mirrorworld guise. The short cropped hair framed a face where the angles were sharper and lines of care creased her brow and bracketed her lips. The white gown whipped in the wind and she looked up at him fondly.

"Need me?" Such a sense of betrayal, guilt, and pain overwhelmed him that Dancer couldn't, for a moment, continue. "Kat, you brought a Mirror to Mere. Don't you understand what that means?"

Her eyes narrowed and he was reminded that she, too, had received a full suite of biotrooper modifications. Kat might seem fragile and languid, but that was illusion. For a moment, in fact, he thought she might attack him, but instead she shook her head.

"Of course I know about the Mirror, Dancer. Do you think Joah and I intended this?"

"I don't understand. Then why have you been trying to lure me to Mere? Why did you bring me to the Mirror?"

"I can't tell you that, Dancer. When will you understand that this is the kingdom of memory, not time?" She sighed. "You have to teach yourself the answer".

"Answer? What answer?"

"Only remember. We love you and we would never willingly bring a Mirror into Mere."

"But— "

Kat disappeared and now Dancer was alone. He tilted his head back to stare up at the stars. Two globular clusters burned where Polaris should be. The lake was filled not with water, but bones. His gaze swept out over a bowl that reached to the horizon. Memory?

Another night, not long after. Floodlights burnished the compound. Sirens blasted the air and Dancer faced his best friend at the threshold of the Mirror. Kat's body was cradled in his arms.

"No, Joah, don't do this."

<In or out, Daniel?>

<Leave Kat with me.>

<Don't follow us.> Joah turned to enter the Mirror. More guards were coming. The die was cast.

<Leave Kat.>

<That's the one thing I can't do, Dancer. You're the only one who can save her.>

He leapt into the Mirror.

Dancer stared at the silvery surface of the portal to another world, a one way journey away from everything he loved. Well, not everything. Then, he thought again about what Joah had said, and finally, he understood why he'd been brought to Mere.

Before anyone could stop him, Dancer jumped into the Mirror, too.

◄⑧ ⑧►

Again, he stood before the Mirror of Mere. But now, wasn't there just the faintest hint of silver, deep in the core of blackness?

He looked down on Joah, still kneeling at his feet, clutching his throat, but a look of triumph danced in his marvelous glowing eyes. Dancer glanced at Kat and back to Joah.

<Does she know?>

<Not yet. She thinks we can all be free.>

Dancer knelt down beside his friend as Kat ran toward them both. Behind him, he heard the faintest breath of wings.

<Isn't there something—>

<No, my friend.> They communed for a heartbeat, sharing their mutual understanding of the terrible windows and the power of shame and hate to warp the soul.

There was so much more he wanted to say, but he could see from Kat's expression of sudden horror that she was hearing everything they said and that she, too, finally understood.

Joah levered himself up with Dancer's help and, without even a backward glance, he stepped into the Mirror, though he sent back one brief thought before he disappeared into his own terrible memories, lost forever.

<Well, ain't this bright?>

Kat dug her fingers into Dancer's arm and her mental cry was shattering. She would have followed him into the Mirror, too, if Dancer hadn't held her back. He had a fleeing thought of what it might be like if both he and Kat joined Joah. The three of them would have all the memory of Mere to wander for eternity together. But the Mirror would remain. And the child would never be born.

The Mirror vanished and in that moment, Mere itself trembled. Kat said nothing, still staring where the Mirror had been.

"You knew. You let him go without me."

Was it hatred in that voice? He thought it might be. But there was no time now for that grief. Mere, always more an idea than a reality, was trembling through time. What was holding the city still? Why hadn't it vanished with Joah, destroying Dancer and Kat where they stood?

Dancer glanced around and saw an ael, with red hair and a blue scarf, arms spread and face tilted to the sky. Kat turned and this time, there was no doubt that she saw him, too.

<Will you be with them? Will you join the Greater Now?>

But the ael only sent the image of Kat and Dancer together, far from this valley. And rainbows.

Dancer took a moment to look into Kat's eyes, both hard and bleak. There was nothing else to say. He led them out of Mere, which was wavering out of existence. Crowds of aels flowed around them, their fur all the colors of all the seasons. The memory of Mere was ending.

They ran as Mere died.

Finally, Dancer carried Kat in his arms and ran faster than he'd ever run in his life.

If Mere fell before they got out of the gates…

Just a little further, he told himself. The old mantra. *Just a little further. Goodbye, Joah, my friend. Just a little further. Farewell, Henge. May you be reborn in the Now. Just a little further. I'm sorry, Kat. I'm sorry. Just a little further. Just a little further…*

◄8 8►

It was Kat who chose their way after, made their camps, found their food, and cooked it. Dancer was unable to see anything clearly at all. He was lost in the habit of memory, unable to connect. Days would pass when he stared into nothingness, or held conversations with the air. Kat fed him, bathed him, led him out of the valley. But she had no maps, no supplies, no real direction. Also, as the weeks passed, the life inside her began to grow and she was forced to think of hard choices. There came a time when she was faced with the decision of continuing on alone, with at least the slim hope of survival for her and the child, or trusting that Dancer might find a way out of the maze of memory that trapped him before it was too late for all of them.

◄8 8►

While Kat led them out into the physical world, Dancer desperately struggled in the Now.

Mere was falling, had fallen, like an enormous house of cards. It was necessary. The Mirror couldn't be allowed to exist. Henge, the guardian, had chosen to destroy the fabulous legacy of his people rather than let it be the vehicle for a cancer. But Dancer refused to accept that choice.

The fragmented sight that Joah had created inside Dancer's mind still held the entirety of Dancer's sojourn as Dancer-Henge and in that precious, fragile multiplicity of memory, perhaps something could be salvaged.

At first, Dancer only worked to remember specific moments of Henge's life, but as each memory linked to another, he began to see how the Now might be remade. But he needed help and Joah was gone.

He called to Kat, mind to mind. And she came.

<Do you see what we have to do?>

<I see…but Dancer, what if reweaving the Now of Mere brings the Mirror back?>

<It can't, Kat. The Mirror was part of Joah's Then and it died with him.>

She tried to hide her grief and anger at Dancer, but in the mental link, there could be no secrets between them.

<I'm sorry, Kat.>

<No, I understand. You had to do it. Joah made you.>

Dancer could have left it at that. It was almost true. But if he had learned nothing else from Joah and Henge it was that self-deception corrupted. If he was going to rebuild a piece of Mere, he wanted to begin the work with a clean heart.

<Joah didn't force me, Kat. I could have refused. But it had to be done. He couldn't be healed. I couldn't live with what you did in Looking Glass. I couldn't let it ever happen again.>

She was silent for a time.

<We didn't know, Dancer. I swear it. Joah only discovered the truth when it was too late.>

As he probed her mind, he saw that she was telling the complete truth. Joah lied, used the lie to drive him, to give him a larger purpose. In the end, though, whether they'd known or not, mattered little to those who died. It mattered to him, though. Dancer's heart lifted.

<Are you ready?>

<Yes.>

The two of them began to fuse Henge's memories into a thread. Kat chose the memories, helping Dancer sort them from the delusions, while Dancer wove. It felt like sewing a gigantic quilt with a needle the size of an atom and each stitch had to be perfect. Many times, Dancer wondered whether what they were trying to do was any use, but Kat kept grimly working and it became clear to him that she was trying to weave a bit of redemption out of the cloth of Mere's memory.

They wove on and on for what might have been days, or an eternity, but the cloth of memory was only a shared idea between them. It lacked the dynamic movement of Mere, the sense of a powerful Now that might be added to and made greater.

Finally, exhausted, the link between them weak and tenuous, Dancer was almost ready to give up. He had failed Henge, as he had failed his mother, as he had failed to save Joah. The buzzing of bees was loud in his ears. It was so tiring screening out those horrible memories. The memory of Henge, with is unshakable faith in the Now, was a pallid construction, lifeless, simply a tapestry of static images of an ael's life.

<Dancer?> Kat's mental voice was as weak as death.

<I know. We've failed. We'll have to break the link. I think our physical selves may be dying and you, well, you have two lives to consider.>

<I've been thinking. There's one set of memories of Henge that we haven't included.>

<?>

<Of the two of you. He was your friend and you shared so much. Don't you think that friendship should be part of his Now?>

Dancer thought about it. He'd felt such guilt over his part in the destruction of Mere, even though he knew rationally that it had to be done, that he hadn't even considered adding their memories. But now that he thought of it, would he have been willing to lose even one memory of Joah, despite everything? Wasn't it the texture of a life that made it live? The mirror of time wasn't memory, but life, all of life.

<Yeah. Yeah, I think you're right.>

The two of them used the last of their mental strength to weave in the chaotic weeks that the human and the ael shared. Dancer remembered every moment, the shock of their first meeting, the joy of the caravan Road, the long days of conversation and friendship on the trail to Taii. He didn't shrink from the madness and fear. With Kat's help, he made sense of them, made them part of the thing they'd built.

And, with the memory of the caravan Road, this fragile Now began to sing of its memory of the Greater Now.

The song was only a small thing now, but it held the heart soaring power of the wedding song. It was strong. The first tiny stone of a new Mere was laid.

❧ 8 ☙

Dancer stared into a campfire. Which one of a thousand fires was this? The Now was with him, like a lover's gift. He saw a figure on the other side. Her cheeks were sunken and the eyes looked filmy. There were new lines in her face and old grime in the lines. She was skinning some kill. They had spent the last few days traveling slowly, aimlessly. But now, at last, Dancer knew where they were.

"Kat?"

She didn't even look up. "Hm?"

He looked at her, this strained and weary woman, who was carrying life inside her, the possibility of new rainbows of memory, a more complete Now.

"There's a caravan trail near here, I think," he said. "I think I can find it."

She looked at him with a mixture of hope and some other emotion that he couldn't quite identify and he didn't dare try to touch her mind. Would she ever forgive him for sending Joah to a death so endless? Would she ever forgive herself?

"Where should we go?" she said, in a flat voice.

"There's a farm community a few weeks hike…where do you want to go, Kat? I'll take you anywhere. I'll never leave you, unless you tell me to."

She looked up. There was no smile. Almost no hope.

"I want to go…will you take me back to Looking Glass?

I want to…" she spread her hands, now grimed with the blood of a small animal. Her voice caught. "I don't know."

"Yeah," said Dancer. He came around to her side of the fire and tentatively drew her close. She resisted a little, but finally let her head rest against his shoulder. She felt so light and thin. "If you try hard enough, you can start over, you know. Wherever we go, from now on, we'll be building Mere."

She gave a dry laugh.

"Well," she said. "Ain't that bright?"

 The End

UNOBEU
United Nations Organization Biological Engineering Unit

MIRRORWORLD
PROJECT

UNOBEU
BIOTROOPER DOSSIER

NAME: Daniel "Dancer" Vicksburg
BIRTHPLACE: Denver, Colorado
DOB: 1/19/78
HEIGHT: 188 centimeters
WEIGHT: 91 kilograms
EYES: Gray

PERSONAL INFORMATION: Youngest son of a middle-class family of grocers, Dancer joined the United Nations Special Program (UNSP) for civilian volunteers right out of school, hoping to take advantage of the program's educational incentives to pay for college. A runner and marathoner, he grew up hiking in the Rockies with his family.

BIOTROOPER ENHANCEMENTS:
Telepathy, stamina, strength, endurance.

NO FURTHER INFORMATION AVAILABLE
THROUGH UNSECURED ACCESS LINE (09)

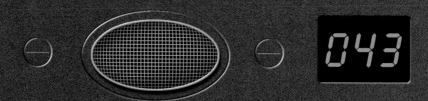

UNOBEU
BIOTROOPER DOSSIER

NAME: Joah "Goldeneyes" Cray
BIRTHPLACE: El Paso, Texas
DOB: 3/12/75
HEIGHT: 177 centimeters
WEIGHT: 75 kilograms
EYES: Gold

PERSONAL INFORMATION: Son of a Border Patrol officer and a schoolteacher, he grew up smart and fast in the political and cultural hotbed of the Texas/Mexico border. Left home young, went to college on a scholarship. Lost many friends and family members to the Bugs and volunteered for the UNSP. The surgery involved in the biotrooper program left him seriously unbalanced—he crossed the Mirror without authorization, kidnapping another trainee. He is an outlaw, a sociopath, and considered to be extremely dangerous.

BIOTROOPER ENHANCEMENTS:
Telepathy, improved reflexes, memory, and strength.

NO FURTHER INFORMATION AVAILABLE
THROUGH UNSECURED ACCESS LINE (43)

UNOBEU
BIOTROOPER DOSSIER

NAME: Katmandu "Kat" Fury
BIRTHPLACE: Bangkok, Thailand
DOB: 6/14/76
HEIGHT: 172.5 centimeters
WEIGHT: 59 kilograms
EYES: Brown

PERSONAL INFORMATION: Child of a U.S. career diplomat and his wife, she lived all over the world as her father moved from post to post. She was a Rhodes Scholar and spent time working for the U.N. in various capacities before the death of her family in a Bug attack prompted her to volunteer for the UNSP.

BIOTROOPER ENHANCEMENTS:
Mental abilities, telepathy, intuition.

NO FURTHER INFORMATION AVAILABLE
THROUGH UNSECURED ACCESS LINE (66)

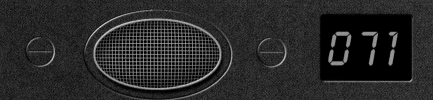

UNOBEU
BIOTROOPER DOSSIER

NAME: David Williams
BIRTHPLACE: Toronto, Ontario, Canada
DOB: 4/4/67
HEIGHT: 192 centimeters
WEIGHT: 97 kilograms
EYES: Brown

PERSONAL INFORMATION: Eldest son of an Alberta ranch family, he was a policeman with a wife (Karen) and a baby daughter (Terry). He volunteered for the USNP when his wife and child crossed the Mirror. He hoped to find and protect them.

BIOTROOPER ENHANCEMENTS:
Speed, strength, endurance, agility.

NO FURTHER INFORMATION AVAILABLE
THROUGH UNSECURED ACCESS LINE (71)

UP
HOME
DOWN

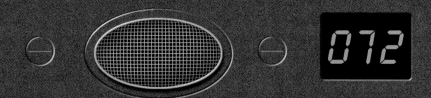

UNOBEU
BIOTROOPER DOSSIER

NAME: Morgan Reaves
BIRTHPLACE: Ann Arbor, Michigan
DOB: 5/8/68
HEIGHT: 185 centimeters
WEIGHT: 86 kilograms
EYES: Blue

PERSONAL INFORMATION: A former big game-hunting guide, Morgan Reaves tested in the top one percent of the applicants for the UNSP. He was assigned to the first wave (Alpha troop) of the forces shipped to Mirrorworld. His assignment on Mirrorworld was to serve as a long-range scout to collect and analyze data.

BIOTROOPER ENHANCEMENTS:
Strength, coordination, heightened healing and immune systems.

NO FURTHER INFORMATION AVAILABLE
THROUGH UNSECURED ACCESS LINE (72)

UNOBEU
BIOTROOPER DOSSIER

NAME: Ryan Carter
BIRTHPLACE: Phoenix, Arizona
DOB: 2/18/64
HEIGHT: 175 Centimeters
WEIGHT: 78 Kilograms
EYES: Brown

PERSONAL INFORMATION: A former U.S. Army Ranger, his aptitude for infiltration and reconnaissance made him a prime candidate for the UNSP. He served as an advance scout for Alpha troop in the first wave of biotroopers to arrive on Mirrorworld.

BIOTROOPER ENHANCEMENTS:
Experimental DNA grafts from a wolf resulted in extreme strength and agility, senses, especially sense of smell, heightened far beyond the norm for biotroopers, claw implants.

NO FURTHER INFORMATION AVAILABLE
THROUGH UNSECURED ACCESS LINE (88)

Serpent in the Garden

Jeremiah Ramson never saw what killed him.
The teenager had been looking for his dog for the past
hour, intent on only two things, the faint tracks in front of
him and the rapidly encroaching sunset. He was well
aware of the clobbering that awaited him if he didn't
get back in time for evening chores.
Jeremiah made sure his bone knife was secure in the
sheath on his braided leather belt. Touching its carved
handle made him feel better, especially since he
knew he wasn't supposed to be here.

WRITTEN BY
John Helfers
ILLUSTRATED BY
Robin Cline

The clan elders had ruled that the foothills were off limits. The official word was that someone might break their leg or be buried by a rockslide. But Jeremiah had heard rumors of a party of men that had traveled into the foothills and never returned. On cold winter nights, it was said that their voices could be heard across the plains, trying to lure unwary clansmen to their deaths. Jeremiah's father had always dismissed the claims as superstitious nonsense, and Jeremiah had always agreed. Until he found himself out here, alone.

However, even with his fear, Jeremiah felt something else. The excitement of exploring unknown territory tingled in his blood. He was always the first one to volunteer to go hunting or foraging, or for any task which let him wander through this strange new world the clan lived in now. There was so much waiting to be discovered here. *Including*, he thought tiredly, *my dog*. Jeremiah needed to find Scout soon so he could head back to the compound and claim that they had gone for a walk. It would be partly true, at any rate.

A rustling in the light blue bushes to his left broke through his thoughts. "Scout? Come here, boy," Jeremiah called. No answer.

Jeremiah drew his knife and edged into the forest, every sense alert. Branches slapped at his legs as he walked. He smelled a rank odor that grew stronger the farther he went. After a couple dozen steps, he came upon a small open space in the brush.

In the clearing was the remains of an animal, so mauled that at first Jeremiah couldn't make out what it had been. As he moved closer, he saw the braided leather collar, a smaller twin to the belt he wore. From that collar hung a piece of wood with a name carved in it.

"Scout." The word caught in his throat. He was still standing there when the bushes behind him exploded in a shower of leaves. Jeremiah felt an incredible pressure on his neck, a flash of pain, and then nothing.

Morgan looked down the rough road for what seemed like the thousandth time. From his vantage point, he could see a good half-mile in either direction. No one coming, no one going. The hot sun made the landscape shimmer before his eyes, turning the sparse grass and packed dirt into smears of green and brown.

Far off in the distance, he could see a smudge of black on the horizon. That was one of the scattered cities of this world, a place called Darklea. Morgan knew he could expect no help from its citizens. After all, they were the ones who had put him here.

Morgan had come to Darklea hoping to find answers to his questions. It turned out that the people of Darklea didn't like questions. Any questions.

When he had been caught, they had taken him before their leader, a man shrouded in darkness save for his gleaming yellow eyes. This man, the one they had called "Father," had looked at Morgan and whispered five words:

"Make an example of him."

And so they had. Morgan gathered his waning energy and strained against the rough ropes that bound him to the cross by the road. A fresh wave of pain assaulted his body as he struggled. The slight space he had given himself by flexing his wrists as they had tied him was gone, taken by the coarse rope as it had absorbed his sweat. He had tried to chafe his wrists raw in hopes that the blood would let him slip free, but that had failed as well. The ropes had drunk his blood as greedily as they had his sweat, and were now swollen around his wrists so tightly he could barely feel his fingers.

His captors had left him a pole to stand on, but it wasn't out of kindness. They wanted to prolong his suffering past the limits of human endurance. The top of the pole tapered to a point. Morgan could stand on it, but only when he gripped it with his bare feet.

After a while, his feet would get tired and he would slip off the pole. This would cause him to fall, closing his throat and chest and and making it impossible to breathe. So he would wearily scramble for a foothold, and the cycle would continue. At least, it would continue until his feet grew too tired to grip the pole, or he grew too tired to lift his legs up anymore. And Morgan was so tired.

So this is where it ends, he thought, *stuck all alone on a cross in the middle of an alien land. The biblical allegory would actually be quite amusing if it wasn't me up here. After all, I've done absolutely nothing to make this a better place. I can't even save myself, much less anybody else.*

Morgan shook his head, desperately trying to dispel his train of thought. Wearily he dragged his left foot back onto the pole, feeling wood slivers pierce his flesh. He tried shaking the cross to see if he could snap one of the wooden pegs that held the cross-piece to the trunk. As he struggled, Morgan wondered how much effort had gone into the making of the dozens of crosses lining the road, many still containing the remains of other "criminals." Effort that could have been put to other, more humane uses.

Of course, if Father had a humane bone in his body, he wouldn't have Darklea under his thumb, Morgan thought, resting for a moment. He felt his feet slipping again, and knew he wouldn't last too much longer. By now he lacked the strength even to hold his head up.

The last sound he heard before fading into unconsciousness was the thump of something hitting the cross. He felt pain as his head was pulled up by his hair, then a high-pitched voice spoke.

"He's alive."

Morgan awoke to find himself lying in a clean bed. His shirt was gone. He'd been washed, and his abraded wrists had been cleaned and bandaged.

"Well, I'd say he's awake now." The voice made him look up.

Six people surrounded his bed, watching him with expressions ranging from guarded to curious. His rescuers were both male and female, ranging in age from a child of about twelve to a bearded man in his early sixties. The one who had spoken was a heavy-set woman with the assured air of a physician. They were all garbed in plain clothing of blue and black, the men in long-sleeved shirts and black pants, the women in dark blue blouses and matching long skirts. They all stared at him silently, as if he was something they had never seen before.

Morgan leaned back against the pillow, content to watch them watch him. After a few seconds the old man whispered to the others around the bedside and all save him and the older woman left, most of them casting backward glances at him as they filed out of the room.

The woman spoke first. "How do you feel?"

"Like I'd been hanging on a cross for a day," Morgan replied.

"Humph," she grunted. "That was two days ago. You've been resting here since we found you."

"Where's here?" Morgan asked.

"The community of Freehaven," the older man said.

"Freehaven?" Morgan thought back through his travels. "I've never heard of anyplace called that here."

The woman smiled. "You might say we're off the beaten path. We're a small agricultural town."

"Mennonites or Amish?" Morgan asked.

"We follow the old ways of cultivating the earth, and are provided for in turn," the old man said. "If you are feeling up to it, you may join us for the evening meal."

Morgan tensed at his commanding tone but was interrupted by the doctor before he could retort.

"All right, let's have a look at those wrists." The old man remained where he was until the woman looked up at him. "Josiah, clear out and let me tend to my patient."

Morgan dutifully extended his arms as he watched the old man leave. The doctor continued speaking. "Don't mind him, he's more than a little set in his ways."

Morgan smiled. "I'd guess he's not the only one."

She looked up at him from her examination and matched his grin. "Well, a lot of things may have changed over here, but my bedside manner hasn't. Now, let's see how you're coming along." She unwrapped the bandages from his forearms and stopped when she saw his wrists.

The skin hardly showed a mark where the ropes had bound him. Samantha gently prodded the area and asked Morgan if it hurt. He shook his head. She looked at his arms and shoulders and asked him to raise them. Morgan did so. After a few seconds, he put them down. He knew why she was staring.

"I'm a quick healer," he said.

She snorted. "You may call that quick. I called it damned miraculous. Two days ago your wrists were chafed to the bone. All the muscles in your shoulders and arms were strained to their limit. It's a wonder you didn't dislocate your shoulders up there."

Morgan shrugged. "All better now," he said. The look on her face told him he hadn't convinced her. He was groping for something else to say when his stomach rumbled loudly enough to make her smile again.

"I'll bet you're hungry. Dinner should be ready soon. Someone will come for you."

"Thank you, Doctor…?"

"Samantha Chappell. And yourself?"

"Morgan. Just Morgan."

She didn't even pause. "You might want to clean up before dinner. I've left water and washcloths on the table. Clothes, too, although whether they'll fit is anyone's guess."

"Thank you."

She nodded and left. Morgan stretched his arms out again, luxuriating in the movement. He threw back the covers, then he realized he was naked. He got out of the bed and padded to the table. A polished wooden bowl of water sat next to a pile of dark blue and black clothes. Morgan splashed water over his face and scrubbed himself, then dressed. The shirt sleeves were a bit short, so he rolled them up past his elbows. The trousers fit better, and the soft moccasins were practically heaven on his feet after what he'd been through.

Once he was dressed, Morgan walked to the room's only window. The last rays of the setting sun illuminated several buildings which looked similar, from what he could see, to the one he was in. Against the sun he saw a long, flat-roofed building with identically-dressed men coming out of it in small groups. They, along with women and children from the various houses, all appeared to be heading for the building Morgan was in. He turned from the window and busied himself tidying up the room.

He had just finished making the bed when there was a knock at the door. "Come in," he said.

The young boy who had been with the group watching him earlier entered. "I'm s'pposed to tell you supper's ready."

Something about the boy's voice was familiar. "You're the one who found me on the cross."

The boy smiled and nodded.

"What's your name?" Morgan asked.

The boy looked at the floor. "Benjamin."

Morgan smiled, happy to have a reason to. "Thanks, Benjamin. I owe you one."

The boy's grin widened until Morgan thought his face would split. He motioned for Morgan to come with him, then turned and left. Morgan followed.

The large room he entered was bustling with activity, most of it centered around the two massive tables that stretched to the far end of the hall. Wooden bowls and platters of food were being carried out by several women, while what appeared to be members of several families trooped in the front door.

Benjamin led Morgan to a chair at one end of the nearest table. Morgan remained standing, aware that his presence was attracting attention. Though no one spoke openly, Morgan could pick out bits of several whispered conversations, and he knew he was the subject.

The smells wafting from several of the plates on the table aroused such hunger in him that he gripped the back of his chair, leaning on it for support. He tried to look like he was relaxing, but from the stares from the men, he didn't think he had pulled it off. The old man, Josiah, walked to his place at the end of one of the tables. The remaining men and women started filing towards chairs. The old man nodded, and the entire group sat down together. As he did so, Morgan noticed one empty space at the second table. He estimated that the entire population of the town, if this was it, numbered about fifty, including several small children and three babies, one of whom couldn't take its bright blue eyes off of Morgan.

The baby set the tone for the entire meal. Every time a dish was passed, no matter where in the room it was, the bearer would casually glance towards Morgan's chair. Morgan ignored the looks and concentrated on the food, much of which he'd never seen before in Mirrorworld. There were some unidentifiable spicy greens, loaves of fresh-baked bread glazed with melted butter, and a thick casserole with a pink vegetable that tasted like potato and chunks of some kind of white meat. It all seemed to agree with him, so Morgan didn't waste time speculating on where it had come from.

One of the first rules he'd learned in Mirrorworld was to eat whatever and whenever he could, for he never knew when his next meal might be. By the looks of these people, they didn't have that problem.

About halfway through the dinner, there was a knock at the main doors. A young man entered and walked to Josiah, who stopped eating. Morgan saw Josiah's eyes flick to the empty space at the table during the whispered conversation, then quickly look away. Morgan noticed the youth's shirt was dark under the shoulders, as if he had been sweating. Or running. Josiah whispered a few more words, then dismissed the man, who left the room. Josiah resumed eating as if nothing had happened.

Morgan continued eating as well, refilling his plate for the fourth time. His appetite was drawing even more attention now, and looks among the townspeople communicated their amazement. Morgan kept on, however, and didn't lay his fork down until the plate had been scraped clean. Not surprisingly, he was the last one to finish. He looked up in time to see just about everyone look away from him.

Josiah bowed his head, followed by every town member. Morgan followed suit, hoping they weren't going to recite anything. After a few minutes of silence, everyone seemed to finish, and they started to leaving the table in small groups, the conversation level rising as they did so. Morgan headed for the main doors, anxious for some fresh air after his large meal.

Outside, a cool breeze was blowing across the town square. Morgan found a spot near the doors and sat down, relishing the calm night. On the far side of the square, a door to one of the houses opened and several figures came out, heading back towards the main building. Morgan was able to hear part of their conversation as they came closer.

"Doctor, Josiah says this was just an isolated incident."

"I don't care what he says, until we find out what did this, we've all got to be more care—" The speaker, Samantha, stopped when she saw Morgan. She looked at the men around her, nodded to them, and watched them head back into the main building.

"Something wrong?" he asked.

"One of our children had an accident. He's dead."

"I'm sorry," Morgan said.

"Apparently he had gone into the foothills, which can be dangerous. Looks like something found him up there," she said.

Morgan's stomach clenched. "Any idea what did it?"

Samantha snorted. "You forget where you are. We barely know half of the creatures around here, even after nine years."

"You've been here that long?" Morgan asked.

"That's what Josiah says. No doubt he's right. I joined up with them about four years ago."

Morgan smiled. "No offense, but you don't seem like the humble religious type."

She wiped her brow. "That obvious, huh? Josiah and his group came here seeking the freedom to practice their religion in peace. I think they were afraid that the modern world would encroach on their way of life until it was eradicated."

"So they come here and the cycle begins again. Aren't they afraid of Father and Darklea coming in and taking over?" Morgan asked.

"Well, I'm sure he's aware of us. But when I was in Darklea about a year ago, Father was too wrapped up in trying to take over either Looking Glass or Shades, I forget which one, to care about us. Is he still at it?"

Morgan shrugged. "I didn't really get a chance to check out the political scene. It wouldn't surprise me if he wanted both of them. When we met, I didn't get a chance to ask him anything."

Samantha's eyebrows rose. "You actually met him?"

"Well, not exactly. The guards threw me down in front of him. Apparently he took a dislike to me, and the rest of the story is pretty easy to figure out." Morgan stretched out his arms.

The short woman nodded. "Uh, yeah. What were you doing there anyway?"

"Looking for someone," Morgan said.

Samantha didn't press. "But as to what you said earlier, he's left us alone so far. His lust is for technology, so we really don't have a lot to offer him. We raise crops and herd animals. If he overfarms the lands near to him, he might annex us for food production, but right now we bother no one."

"And you seem to be doing pretty well here," Morgan said, looking around.

"Say what you want about this world, but to these people, this is the promised land," Samantha said.

"Where they can live in peace," Morgan said. "Hopefully it will stay that way."

She nodded, then stepped toward the doors. "I'd better report to Josiah. I think you'll be staying in the same room you were in before. Get some rest," she said.

"Yes, Doctor." Morgan watched her enter the hall. *If Father stretched forth his arm, and told his minions, "Go forth and conquer," this place would be toast in an hour,* he thought. *So why hasn't he?* From what Morgan had seen of Father, he wasn't the type to ever be content with what he had. *We bring with us whatever we can to Mirrorworld,* he thought, *including tyrants.* Shaking his head, Morgan felt himself growing sleepy. *Maybe things will make more sense in the morning,* he thought. He had lost count of how many times he had thought that, only to awaken to new chaos with each day.

Morgan walked through the dining hall to his room and closed the door. Sliding out of his shirt and pants, he fell onto the bed and was asleep within minutes.

Morgan's eyes snapped open, and it was a few seconds before he realized where he was. The pale yellow light of the nightly borealis streamed in through cracks in the shuttered windows, bathing the room in a ghostly glow.

What woke me? he thought. He lay in bed and listened. All was quiet. Yet he couldn't shake the feeling that something was wrong. *A noise...something like wood banging against wood.* He strained his ears, but still heard nothing.

That's one of the problems in Mirrorworld, he thought, *no night noise.* The insect life here was quiet during the evening hours.

He got out of bed and dressed, figuring he'd take a stroll around the square as long as he was awake. He crossed the empty dining hall to the main entrance and stepped outside, easing the doors shut behind him.

The night was just as he had left it, calm with a slight breeze. Morgan was trotting down the steps, marveling at the peacefulness he felt here, when another noise caught

his attention. Scanning the square, Morgan quickly found the source. One of the shutters on a nearby house was swinging in the wind, occasionally thudding against the side of the building. Morgan recognized the noise that had awakened him earlier. Walking over to the window, he saw the only thing wrong with it was a broken catch. He took a small stick lying on the ground nearby and propped the shutter open.

Just as he finished testing his work, Morgan noticed a rank odor coming from inside the house. He looked inside, but saw nothing out of the ordinary. *Maybe one of their pets left a "present" for the household*, he thought.

Morgan turned to leave when he was jerked off his feet and slammed against the side of the house. What felt like a band of iron was locked around his throat, making breathing impossible, let alone yelling for help.

The smell was overpowering now. *Who the hell is this?* Morgan strained to pry the restraining arm away from his throat. It didn't budge. *Whoever it is, it's human.* Morgan's feet drummed against the side of the house as he felt his head being pulled through the open window.

Through the pounding of his blood in his ears, Morgan heard a sibilant snuffling behind him. He let go of the arm and flailed wildly through the window. Through his panic Morgan heard the clack of teeth snapping. He reached farther back, and encountered what felt like filthy, matted hair. He tried to grab hold, but it slipped through his sweating fingers. *Can't get...any leverage. Damn, I'm going to...die for being a...Peeping Tom.*

Spots were swimming before Morgan's eyes now, and he knew he was going to black out any second. He thrust his arm back again. This time his flailing fingers found something soft and jelly-like. Morgan clawed at it with all his remaining strength

An agonized howl split the night air. The arm released Morgan, who fell to the ground under the window, gasping for breath. The howls continued, punctuated by the sounds of splintering wood and broken pottery. *What the hell is in there, and why did it come after me?*

Morgan hauled himself upright, careful to stay well away from the window. By now he could hear noises of other clan members coming to investigate what was happening. Morgan staggered around the side of the house to the front door and reached for the carved wooden handle. Just as his fingers touched it, the world exploded around him.

Morgan's eyes fluttered open. He saw he was back in his bedroom, a familiar face hovering over him.

"Haven't we done this once already?" he asked Samantha. It hurt even to say those few words. He started to sit up, but was stopped by Sam's hand on his shoulder.

"Easy, Morgan, you're not going anywhere. You're lucky to be alive."

"What happened?" he asked.

"By the time we got there, it was pretty much all over. One of the men saw something he described as 'a demon from hell,' crouched over you. He shouted, and it looked up, saw the men coming, sprang to the roof of the house and was gone."

"What about the family in that house?" Morgan asked.

Samantha looked at the floor. "Dead. All of them torn apart just like Jeremiah." Morgan leaned back against the pillow and sighed. Samantha continued. "Why are you still alive, Morgan?"

He frowned. "Probably because your men scared the thing off before it had a chance to kill me."

Sam shook her head. "No, I don't think so. Paul, the man who saw the creature, said it was crouched over you, not moving, just staring at your face. If it had wanted to, it could have torn you open in the blink of an eye. But it didn't. Paul said it was as if this thing...recognized you. When I described it just now, you reacted as if you knew it as well."

She leaned forward and stared at Morgan. "You heal faster than any human being has a right to. No one recovers from the kind of wounds you had without permanent scarring. Even now, as we're talking, your voice seems stronger. Who—or what—are you?"

Morgan looked steadily at her. "Do you really want to know?"

Samantha held her eyes steady. "If you're a threat to us, yes I want to know. I think we've earned that right."

Morgan nodded and relaxed a bit. "Yes, you have," he said. "I have to warn you that you're probably not going to like what I have to say."

"Try me," Samantha said.

"I'm an artificially enhanced human," Morgan began. "I was part of a project the United Nations sent through the Mirrors to locate those who had been taken by those alien Bugs. As I'm sure you and the rest of the folks here found out, nothing inorganic survives the trip through the mirrors: no guns, no chemicals, not even tooth fillings. No weapons of any kind. So they took volunteers from around the world and augmented them into weapons. Some of us were enhanced with heightened intelligence, with photographic memories capable of storing complicated diagrams and schematics, so when we got over here, and with the proper materials, we could construct what would be needed. Others, such as myself, were enhanced physically. They boosted my immune system and and heightened my senses. I was to be an advance scout for the group, at least, what was left of us."

"What do you mean by that?" Samantha asked.

"Only about half survived the training and augmentation process. Those who survived, well, it's hard to say really, but there was a kind of bond between us all. I think that's why whoever was out there didn't kill me." Morgan said.

"You mean—that—thing was one of you?" Sam asked.

"Yeah." Morgan sighed. "We had no idea what they were going to do to us. I'm surprised that any of us lived through it. The programs were mainly experimental. Sometimes there were...accidents. For example, one night I woke up hearing odd noises in my room. Little clicking sounds, like someone was rolling dice. I turned on the light switch to find my roommate biting his fingers off, one joint at a time. The clicking noise was the sound of his fingerbones hitting the floor after he'd cleaned the meat off. After the soldiers came and took him out of there, I never saw him again."

"And what's been killing us is part of this project?"

Morgan nodded. "*Was* part of the project. Once the remaining project members came here, only a few actually continued the original mission. I was one of them. One morning I woke up to find the rest of the group gone. They didn't leave, they just vanished. That was a long time ago. I've been looking for them ever since. I got on the trail of whatever it is out there back west. I've been tracking him for the past three or four months. He was the reason I was asking questions in Darklea."

"Goddammit, it would have been nice if you had told us this earlier. There's a family dead out there because you didn't!" Samantha said.

"How was I supposed to know he'd wind up here? I trailed him to Darklea and lost him there. He could have struck out in any direction. He's never hit any kind of settled area before. Do you think I wanted this to happen!"

Samantha turned and stalked to the doorway.

"Doctor, wait," Morgan said. Samantha stopped at the door but didn't turn. "I need your help. Look, what just happened to that family was a tragedy, and no one's more sorry than I am, but now we've got to stop it from happening again. I can't do it alone. Please help me."

She looked back over her shoulder at him. "What do you want to you do?"

Morgan's answer was short. "Trap him, interrogate him, and kill him."

She hesitated. "I'll have to speak with the others. Don't worry, I won't tell them everything. Right now I just want to stop him before more people die." She started to open the door.

"Sam," Morgan said, "you know if there was any way I could have prevented what happened tonight, I would have."

She looked at him, nodded, and left the room.

Morgan stared at the ceiling. *I always thought it would be so easy when I found him, but what if I can't do it? Even though he's murdered who knows how many people, if he recognized me, then maybe there's a chance he could be saved? Maybe he knows where the others are.* He shook his head. *Get real. Even if we did manage to capture him alive, what would we do? He's more animal than man now. He'll never stop until everyone here is dead. It'll be more of a mercy killing than anything. I just hope Samantha isn't turning the whole town against me right now.*

"You're going to do what?" Morgan couldn't believe his ears. It was the next morning, and although Morgan had been feeling a bit better, the conversation he was having with Josiah was not helping his mood.

"You heard me. We will do absolutely nothing to help you," Josiah replied.

"This...thing has now killed five of your group. That family last night, and the boy in the mountains earlier. It won't stop until you're all dead. You're isolated and defenseless. This place is just a giant smorgasbord to it."

"Be that as it may, violence will not solve the problem."

Well, there's only one other solution," Morgan said. "It'll move on when every man, woman, and child here has been killed."

"If the Lord wills it, then so shall it be done," Josiah said. Morgan could not even summon up a retort, partly because of his injuries and partly because he was so amazed he could barely think. Josiah stood near his bed, watching him.

"You're sentencing every person in this village to death. You know that, don't you?" Morgan said.

"The Lord works in mysterious ways," Josiah replied without a trace of irony. He turned and walked out, closing the door behind him.

Morgan dropped his head back onto the pillow, exhaling loudly. "Sam? You know how Josiah thinks?"

She nodded.

"He's not going to change his mind, is he?"

She shook her head.

"And his decision is final, I mean, no one is going to defy him, right?"

She shook her head again.

Morgan shook his head. "So this is what Gary Cooper felt like. God, these people won't even lift a finger to save themselves. It's over, Sam. This place is gone. If I were you, I'd start packing now."

Samantha looked at her patient for a long time. Then she spoke, quietly and carefully. "Morgan, I don't think you understand how important this is to them. The idea of nonviolence is just as much a part of their life as breathing. They can't just set aside their laws when it's convenient, do what needs to be done. and then pick them back up again. What they're doing takes more courage that you or I may ever have."

Morgan's head snapped around, fury blazing in his eyes. Before he could speak, Samantha continued, "I know what you're going to say, and I agree that what you've been through also takes courage, but think of this: these people came here with no augmentation, no implants, no training. They were simply looking for a place where they could live and worship in peace. This world is their Eden, it's their paradise. And, like the biblical garden, there are serpents."

Morgan tried to interrupt again but was stopped by her raised palm. "And along with those serpents, there are those who will fight them. Josiah has often said that for those who believe, God will provide. Perhaps this time, he's provided you."

As Samantha spoke, the fire slowly left Morgan's eyes. When he spoke, his voice was a little shaky. "Come on, Sam, don't tell me that you're starting to buy into this 'God's will' stuff."

"In the years I've been in Mirrorworld, I've seen acts of unspeakable cruelty and gestures of amazing kindness. Back on Earth I was a card-carrying churchgoer, until my medical practice burned any belief in religion right out of me. I came to this place by accident, and spent the next few years just trying to survive. Then I found these people, who had made a voluntary pilgrimage to an unknown, possibly hostile land. If there is any kind of spiritual force in the universe, it told me to stay with them. I've never regretted it. I believe that you were brought here for a reason. Right now that reason is threatening our entire way of life. You asked me for help earlier, now I'm asking you. Josiah said none of them would help you, but he didn't say that you couldn't try and stop it. Technically, I'm a member of the community, but I can do what I wish. With my help, maybe we can catch him," Samantha said.

Morgan thought over what she had said for a moment. "Even if what you say is true, I'm in no shape to take him on."

"Not necessarily. I didn't tell you that the first victim, the boy, was found yesterday, but had been missing for two days. Your 'creature' apparently gorges himself after he kills and finds somewhere to sleep while he digests. When he's hungry, he wakes up and repeats the process. Now, this is just a guess, but if I'm right, we've got two, maybe three days before he shows up again. If we use that time to heal you and set a trap for him, it's possible we could stop him for good."

Morgan nodded. "Sounds like you've been putting a lot of thought into this, Doc."

"This place is our home, and I'll fight to protect it. I'm going to poke around for whatever might be of use to us. You get some sleep."

"Samantha," Morgan called after her. She stopped. "There aren't a lot of rules I live by in this world, but right now I know one that I'm going to take to heart."

"What's that?" she asked.

"Follow the doctor's orders," Morgan said. She smiled, nodded and walked out. After she was gone, Morgan's face turned serious. *I only hope she can pull some miracle out of her black bag that will even the odds. Right now they're not stacked in our favor.*

They spent the next day coming up with ideas on how to catch the rogue soldier. Samantha and Morgan sifted through outdoor and indoor traps, using his knowledge of survival training and her short list of what was available in the village. Finally they agreed that the man had to be lured into a house, then dealt with.

Surprisingly, the more they discussed what to do, the more Morgan leaned towards trying to take the trooper alive.

"When did you change your mind about killing him?" Samantha asked.

"Well, if he recognized me, and if we can capture him alive, maybe there's a chance he can be helped. Also, he may have the information I'm looking for. I'd like to know either way."

"Those are mighty big ifs," Samantha said. "Luckily I have something that might help." She reached into a belt pouch and brought out a small clay jar. She handed it to Morgan, who looked inside and saw a dark red powder. He started to touch it with his finger, but Samantha stopped him. "Don't touch that."

"What is it?"

"The truth is, I'm not sure. One of the children stumbled into a patch of the plant this came from while picking what passes for flowers out in the fields. She scratched herself on a thorn and was asleep for two days. The merest trace of it—inhaled or in your blood-stream—knocks you out. I use it as an anesthestic for surgery. What do you think?"

"I think I feel a whole lot better about our chances. So, I'll have a needle or pointed stick of some kind and scratch him with it when he comes in, right?"

Samantha shook her head. "Actually, I think it would be better if I did it." Morgan started to protest, but Samantha held up her hand. "Before you say anything, just listen. First, how did this thing find our settlement?"

Morgan thought for a minute. "Logically, he smelled your boy's trail and followed it back here."

"Exactly. Now I'll just bet he got a big noseful of your scent when he was giving you the hairy eyeball last night. If he smells you again wherever we set up, it might give the whole thing away. If that doesn't tip him off, when he sees you there, he might also sense a trap. It's better to have someone there whom he's never seen or smelled before, yes?"

"Yes, but it's too dangerous."

Samantha shook her head. "Even healing as well as you are, you're in no condition to stop anyone. You'll be backup. This'll do the trick," she said, taking the clay jar from him and sealing it shut.

"We hope," Morgan said.

"I haven't seen anything that breathes stand up to this yet."

"Sam, have you ever seen anything like what we're up against?" Morgan asked.

She slowly shook her head. "Good point. I'd better double the normal dose."

"Hell, I'd suggest triple. Too much is never enough in this case." Morgan smiled, then winced as the pain in his ribs flared up.

Samantha bent over him. "How is it?"

"Knitting...just fine, thanks," he said.

"Morgan, are you sure you're up to this?" Samantha asked.

"Absolutely," Morgan lied. "No way am I letting you face that thing alone."

"Good. I was kind of hoping you'd say that."

"Yeah," Morgan said. "Well, we'd better get some rest, 'cause we won't get any tonight."

Samantha nodded. "I'll see you just before dusk. I'll be getting the house ready."

Morgan watched her leave. He leaned back and tried to sleep, but too many thoughts kept whirling through his mind. The cracks in their plan, the things that could go wrong. *Better face facts, there's only Samantha, me, and a little jar of powder between him and the village. That's all we've got, and it's gonna have to do.*

The day passed slowly, and evening crept up on the village. By the time the golden borealis lit the night sky, the town was silent, every door locked, every light out, every window shuttered.

Every window but one.

Morgan exhaled a long, slow breath and tried to relax. Stuck in the cramped attic of the house they had chosen to set their trap in, he felt worse than useless. True, he had a long pole with the drug liberally applied to the pointed end, in case Samantha didn't get the chance to use her stick. He would have to lean over the trap door and stab towards the bed, which they had moved so he'd have a clear shot. They had a coil of strong rope, in case the drug worked. They also had several farm implements, in case the drug didn't work. When Morgan had seen the wickedly curved metal of the pitchfork and sickles, he had smiled and said. "Maybe just the sight of these will make him give up."

"I hope so, because I'm taking one to bed with me." Samantha's grin had made Morgan wince.

That had been hours ago. Now the time for jokes was past. Morgan shifted his weight, trying to find a more comfortable position. He listened carefully, past the noise of Samantha's quiet breathing, past the settling noises of the house, to the sounds outside. He heard nothing.

Waiting is the hardest part, Morgan thought. The noises of the house as it creaked and popped made him jumpy. He couldn't be sure if the sounds he was hearing were made by the house or by something else.

If their visitor went after Sam, he wouldn't get a second chance. Three, four seconds, tops. Then she wouldn't have a prayer.

So concentrate, dammit. He forced his mind back to the present, back to the woman below him risking her life for everyone in the surrounding buildings.

A slight creak caught his attention. Was that the shutter being opened? Morgan held as he tried to hear what was going on outside. Everything was quiet. Even the house had decided to join the silence. Morgan strained his senses to the limit, searching for the slightest noise.

When it came, it wasn't from the direction he had expected. He heard soft rustling from somewhere above him. Morgan saw tiny bits of dried grass drift down as something moved across the thatched roof.

Morgan looked at the far wall where the trooper was apparently headed. In the wall near the roof was a small window for ventilation. *He can't get through that, no one could*, Morgan thought. But as he watched, a hand reached down to grab the vertical cross-piece in the window's center and snap it off. The hand dropped the stick and started working on the horizontal support. The filthy fingers were tipped with sharp claws that bit into the wood before breaking it.

That scared him. *There's no room for me to maneuver in here. I'd be dead in a heartbeat.* Morgan crawled to the ladder and started climbing down to the main room. Another snap from behind him told him he didn't have much time. He paused when he realized he'd left his pitchfork and stick on the floor, but he knew that he couldn't go back for them.

Samantha looked at him questioningly as he crept down the last few rungs. Holding a finger to his lips, he pointed at the hole above him, pointed to her, then pantomimed sleeping. She nodded, lay back, and closed her eyes.

Morgan stole to the far side of the room. As he did so, he saw the small clay jar of anesthetic on the table. He grabbed it and ducked underneath the table. The ache in his ribs flared as he crouched, waiting.

The ladder creaked. Once, then again. It was coming down the rungs. A pungent, musky stench filled the room. Morgan smelled something else as well, an underlying odor of infection. He tensed, waiting for it to reach the floor. Morgan heard the grass mattress rustle as the creature moved onto it. From where he was, Morgan couldn't see a thing. Then he heard something very clearly, something that chilled him to the bone.

"Morgan." The voice sounded like it came out of a throat filled with rocks. "I know you're here. I smelled you upstairs. Come out and she lives a while longer."

Morgan stepped out from underneath the table and stood up, careful to keep the hand with the jar behind him.

The biotrooper was crouched on the bed over Samantha, who was staring up at

134

him. His body was thin yet muscular and covered with a thick coat of hair. His arms were longer than a normal man's, almost ape-like in appearance. One of those arms was over Sam. His hand was at her throat, those terrible claws lightly touching her skin, almost caressing her. The biotrooper looked at Morgan and grinned.

The face of the man that stared back at Morgan looked like a demon from hell. His teeth were long and pointed, encrusted with bits of his last meal. His nose had receded into his face, leaving two small slits for breathing. Shaggy hair sprouted from his head in all directions, with leaves and twigs entangled it. He stared at Morgan with one wide red eye. The other was gone, a blood- and pus-covered hole all that remained. A clear liquid dripped from the socket, carving a white track on the grime-covered face. But for all that, Morgan knew who he was.

"Carter."

The man-thing's eye squinted, then he nodded, his whole body jerking in his excitement. "Yes," he said, drawing out the last syllable like a snake's hiss.

At that moment, Sam moved, plunging her stick into Carter's wrist, who howled and jerked his hand back. He leapt off the bed to the door, but seemed to slip when he landed. As he tried to get up, Morgan saw that he was swaying, unable to right himself. He took a step towards Morgan, then his eye rolled back and he slumped to the floor.

Morgan leaned against the table, pain lancing through his chest. He looked at Samantha, who was sitting upright in the bed.

"You all right?"

She nodded. "I think so." She looked at the unconscious Carter. "Is that what you're going to turn into?"

"Nah," Morgan said. "If I haven't changed yet, I'm not too worried. Come on, we'd better tie him up before he comes to."

"Morgan, you can't possibly think he's going to wake up. There was enough anesthetic on that stick to drop an elephant for a week."

"Maybe, but I'm not taking any chances." Slipping the drug jar into his belt pouch, Morgan stepped over the prone Carter and jerked his hands behind his back. "Once he's secured, we can move him into the main room and decide how to handle this. Toss me the rope, will you?"

Samantha reached down under the mattress for the coil of rope, looking away from Morgan for a few seconds. That was when Carter moved.

His clawed hands shot up and grabbed Morgan's shirt, pulling him down. Carter arched his neck up and slammed the back of his skull into Morgan's jaw hard enough to throw him backwards. By the time Samantha had turned back to Morgan with the rope in her hand, Carter was already on his feet.

Sam scrabbled for her drugged stick, but it was too late. With one bound, Carter leapt straight at her, knocking her squarely into the wall. Sam didn't make a sound as she slid down to the floor, unconscious.

Using his impact with Samantha as energy, Carter pushed off the ceiling, and landed on top of Morgan. His claws bit lightly into Morgan's throat. The next words he hissed shocked Morgan into full consciousness.

"Father says you die."

"Why didn't you kill me before? You had the chance." Morgan gasped, barely able to breathe with Carter's weight on his chest.

"I was surprised to find you here, so I reported back. After Father killed the men who were supposed to have taken care of you, he told me to finish the job. Don't think you could have escaped me. I could have killed you any time I wanted to. I just wanted to see what you were capable of. This pathetic trap couldn't have caught a mouse, much less me."

"Your enhancements make you that much better that the rest of us?" Morgan asked. His right hand inched its way towards his belt pouch.

"This has nothing to do with the world we once knew. Here I'm the ultimate predator, stronger and smarter than just about anyone. I hunt the weak, the unfit, those unable to survive. I make the lands stronger, so everyone benefits."

"Uh-huh. And does Father hold the other end of your leash?" Morgan asked.

For a second he thought he has gone too far, but Carter reigned in his temper before his claws ripped through Morgan's throat. "Father is going to rule all of Mirrorworld soon, and I'll be there at his side. You and your stupid farmers will not live to see that day," Carter sneered, his clawed hand tightening around Morgan's neck.

"Maybe not, but can you do one thing before you kill me?" Morgan asked.

"What's that?"

"Shut up!" With that Morgan brought his hand holding the clay jar of anesthetic up and smashed it into Carter's mouth, shattering it. Morgan held his breath as both men's faces were enveloped in a cloud of dark red powder.

Carter, however, inhaled as the drug covered his face, nose, and mouth. He reared back, choking and gasping for air. Morgan pushed Carter off his legs and tried to scramble away from the biotrooper and the cloud of powder. His lungs burned from lack of oxygen. He crawled until his head bumped the wall of the far side of the room. Cautiously Morgan took a breath and immediately felt the drug take hold. He slumped to the floor. The last thing he saw was Carter's body jerking spasmodically across from him.

"Morgan...Morgan, are you awake?"

The blur in front of Morgan's eyes solidified into the face of Samantha. Her head was wrapped in a bandage, but otherwise she looked none the worse for wear.

"Where's Carter?" he asked.

"Dead. His body may have been able to handle a triple dose of that drug, but what you threw at him would kill anybody. You almost didn't make it either."

Morgan nodded. "How are you doing?"

"Just a lump on the noggin for my trouble, thank you. Carter didn't do your ribs any good by sitting on them either. Don't even think of sitting up."

Morgan breathed shallowly. "So the threat is over for now."

Samantha frowned. "What do you mean, 'for now'?"

"Just before Carter was going to kill me, he told me he was sent here on Father's orders. Not only to kill me, but the rest of you as well. Once you were either scared or killed off, the place would be open for his people to take over."

"I don't understand. This is all Father's doing? But why not just come and take over? He's got the manpower and the weapons," Samantha said.

"Perhaps he thought this would be enough to drive you out. He might not want to split his forces if he's trying to move against the other city-states. It would deplete him too much if a serious threat arose somewhere else." Morgan said.

"So now what?"

"Josiah is going to have to pick a side, before it's chosen for him. You can't just sit here in your own little world and hope evil doesn't come knocking on your door. Even if your people are nonviolent, they could help Shades and Looking Glass with food and supplies in exchange for protection."

"Assuming Shades and Looking Glass are any better than Darklea in the first place. I don't know. Maybe it would be better for us to try and negotiate a noninterference treaty, you know, become the Mirrorworld version of Switzerland."

Morgan nodded. "Maybe, but from what Carter said, Father's got big plans, and taking over this place is part of them. Sooner or later, you'll have to defend what you put together here, before it's taken from you."

"And what about you?" Samantha asked.

"What about me?" Morgan said.

"Once you're better, you'll just move on, right?"

Morgan looked at the wall. "Sure, I thought about staying, but where would I fit in? I'm a warrior, not a farmer," Morgan said.

"Will you listen to yourself?" Samantha sighed. "For God's sake, Morgan, this isn't an Eastwood movie where the mysterious hero rides off into the sunset after saving the town. If Father is going to move against us again, we'll need you. There's no reason you can't stay during the interim. You learned to fight, you can learn to farm. Who knows, you may like it here."

"I already like it here, even with Josiah. All right, just for a while, until we see what Father does. Perhaps we should try to sneak into Darklea to find out what he's planning?"

"Why don't we leave the tactics until you're well enough to stand." Samantha replied. "Then we'll worry about Father, all right?"

"Right." Morgan smiled. "Always follow the doctor's orders," he yawned. Within seconds he was fast asleep.

Samantha studied him for a few minutes, then quietly rose and walked to the door. Just before she left, she looked back at him. "For thy power standeth not in multitude nor thy might in strong men; for thou art a God of the afflicted, a helper of the oppressed, an upholder of the weak, a protector of the forlorn. God bless you, Morgan."

With that she quietly shut the door, leaving Morgan to sleep in peace.

❧finis❧

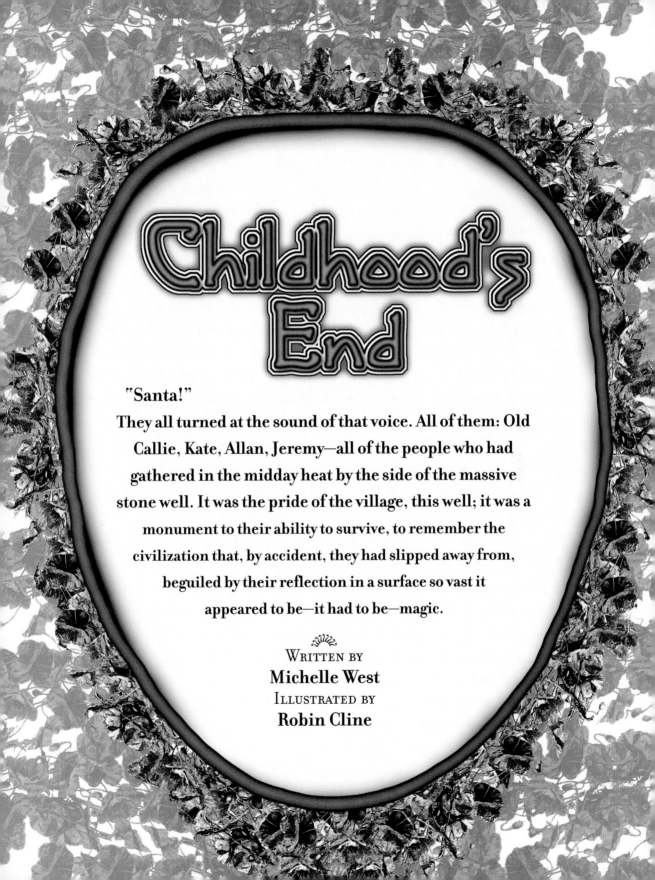

Childhood's End

"Santa!"

They all turned at the sound of that voice. All of them: Old Callie, Kate, Allan, Jeremy—all of the people who had gathered in the midday heat by the side of the massive stone well. It was the pride of the village, this well; it was a monument to their ability to survive, to remember the civilization that, by accident, they had slipped away from, beguiled by their reflection in a surface so vast it appeared to be—it had to be—magic.

WRITTEN BY
Michelle West
ILLUSTRATED BY
Robin Cline

Magic, adventure, surprise—the conjurings of a dark alchemy of the spirit—had lured most of them on. Of course, some people came through because the mirror bisected their daily walk; they were in mid-step and too damned stupid to do anything but pinch themselves hard and try to wake up when they reached the other side. They had a lot of time to think about it afterward—about the ones who had turned around, right away, who'd gone back. All the time in the world, in fact—this world, whatever the hell it was called.

"Uncle Allan! Get Santa!" No one over the age of ten shouted for Santa. No one under that age did unless they were in serious trouble. Jack was only seven—too young to even begin to hide the fear in his voice.

"What the hell?" Allan stepped away from the well, carefully pulling his elbows up from rock still new enough to have sharp edges.

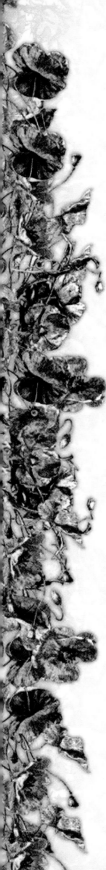

"Jeremy! Get Santa!" Fleet-footed, the boy approached them, mud-speckled and white-skinned in the early spring sun.

The two men exchanged a wary glance.

Allan and Jeremy had been two things when they'd first arrived: the youngest of the men—a thing that had seldom been considered a great advantage in their old life—and the most fanatic members of the "make the SCA *really* historical" faction of their Society of Creative Anachronism group at the University of Toronto.

As Jeremy was quick to point out, the historical period they were aiming at then was European medieval, not incompetent hunter-gatherer. But he managed to say it with humor, and if it was gallows humor, no one complained. They'd come to know how close they were to death in this new world, and anything that pulled them back from its edge helped. Both the knowledge and the humor these two had brought with them had been invaluable. Especially when the people of this new, accidental village—although it had been anything but that in the first few months—had rediscovered the hard truths they'd forgotten they didn't know.

The first few months, they'd spent redefining what the word "hell" meant. And they thought they understood it, until that first death. Among the visitors, which is all that anyone could think of to call such a disparate group of Toronto's former citizens, there had been enough people with camping skills that they all hadn't died immediately. But it was touch and go. No utility knives. No scissors. No food—no packed trail rations, although as Jeremy pointed out, some of them had packed a lunch.

People had laughed at that. Nervous, halting laughter. Better than nothing. But they had no nets or lines for fishing, though until they'd agreed to trek outward in the hope of finding water, that hadn't mattered. It was more of a problem that half of them couldn't see. Glasses—like zippers and buttons and cavity fillings—were lost in transition, obvious victims of the walk through the mirror. There were other losses, too—many of them subtle and slow to surface.

Old Callie had led them to water, so to speak. She'd beaten them all into shape; she was the mother they had all left behind and buried in their subconscious mind—absolute, affectionate, just. She was too cranky and earthy to become a religious figure, and too self-confident to be ignored; in short, a leader.

But there were things even she couldn't face down and scare off—and death was one of them. What the others were, no one was certain, and it was the subject of many a betting pool, all private. Callie had a temper.

Three months after that first day, they lost Linda. It was during what passed for winter around these parts—a pathetic winter at that, given Toronto in the

nineties—that she caught cold. That was all it was: a cold. But she never got better.

It was the first time they'd had to think about using their hard-cleared land for something other than shelter or lame attempts to grow food. Old Callie had made the decision for all of them: the dead had to be honored so the living would remember that they were more than animals. The mourners had to have a place to go to remember—some evidence that a life had existed. She made it mandatory to mourn.

And they did mourn, not just for Linda, but for all they'd lost, for the living who might as well be dead to them. God. It had been hard to bury her. Not one of them had handled a corpse before. Amazing what people could do, given incentive. Given Callie.

Burying Linda, they buried a lot of their past, but it was years before the last of them accepted that *this* was home. It wasn't until the third death that they named the village.

Jackson didn't die of a disease. He got caught in a rock slide that he, Allan, and Jeremy started. They had no quarry, of course, but they'd found two things they needed: Limestone, and an outcropping of jagged rock from which loose boulders—or whatever you called big, heavy chunks of stone—could be pried. Prying was dangerous and time-consuming. They'd thought they could control the rocks' slide.

Best-laid plans of people who'd been shoehorned into a life that didn't fit them.

Jackson's leg was both broken and crushed.

He should have lived, but no one had the sense, the courage, or the stomach to do what was necessary. Cut off a man's leg with a rough stone knife, or a wooden one…his painful, messy death was the consequence.

Jackson's favorite book had been *Childhood's End*. Clarke had—through words on the printed page, no more and no less—given the young Jackson a window into a different world, a world of learning, science, an escape from the religion and superstitions of the small town he'd called home for the first twenty years of his life. He became the first person from his high school to go to college in nearly a decade. He was, had been, an engineer.

Between them—he, Allan, and Jeremy—they'd convinced people to build. To move one step further along the path toward something more than hand to mouth survival. The most important step.

Allan didn't think it fitting to stop that building because of Jackson's death. It was the worst sort of last respect they could pay a man like Jackson, to let his death stop them; so Allan didn't. Didn't let anyone else either; that was the way he showed his respect.

Jeremy insisted that the village be called Childhood's End. Callie had nodded, in silence. It was done.

There were already two children among the people of Childhood's End when the mirrors had closed. Both of them were very young. The first, an infant, was the second person in the village to die. That death almost killed them all; but since Susan, the child's mother, hung on somehow and didn't fall to pieces—at least in public—no one else felt they could. The other child, an older girl, who had toddled her way through the reflective surface of the mirror just that extra inch outside of her mother's reach, survived. Colds, two fevers, poor food outside of the nursing her mother had continued to do—Terry survived all of it.

Her mother, Karen, didn't. The people of Childhood's End learned to say that too damned much. So-and-so didn't make it.

They learned not to think about the deaths. It was life that mattered. Terry changed their lives because the world she lived in was the only world that she really knew; the past and the present didn't exist in the same space for her. She could ask about home, and she did, but the questions were always passing clouds.

Broke their hearts when her mother died and had to be buried. Terry knew that something was wrong because her mother wasn't moving, but she wailed and howled and tried to bite and kick people away from the shallow grave when they finally started laying down the dirt. Susan took her in.

They thought the loss of both parents in one year would scar Terry—and maybe it did—but she was more whole at three than any of the rest of them.

Two more children were born the following year. They survived, but they taught the village of Childhood's End that childbirth was itself deadly: it brought life; it took it. Debbie died. Her child was adopted by the village, and nursed by the woman who bore the town's first baby boy.

It was that boy, Jack—named, as the well was, for the man who had died to make the rocks that formed its walls accessible—who ran toward them now, his bare feet caked in mud.

Allan swore softly. He stepped out onto the warm, flat walkway made of rocks that had also come from that first big slide. Knelt and opened his arms to catch the two-legged projectile. "Whoa!"

Jack was doing a passable imitation of breathing; passable, but not entirely convincing. "Get Santa!" The child's pale hair, tangled with burrs that seemed to grow there, flew from side to side as he struggled for enough air to form words. "Some strangers up by Apple Creek have trapped Terry up a tree!"

No one asked any questions.

They split at once, the people at the well, running through the packed dirt that passed for a street as they searched for Santa. Strangers came in a variety of flavors on this world, all of them desperate. Some were easier to handle then others. Santa had been a stranger once, and he never let them forget it. Not with his words, but with his silence. He was a hard man to like—unless there was an emergency.

Old Callie had once asked him what he'd done for a living in his previous life. If he'd answered at all, no one else knew what he'd said, and she wasn't telling. Which meant it had to be bad; Callie wasn't the tactful sort. She'd have said something about any occupation short of serial killer.

"Hey, Jeremy—" a woman called.

"No time. Seen Santa?"

Susan's face fell, or rather the lift of her cheeks that was all smile did. "I think he's with the cows."

"Great. And the cows?"

"He herded them down lakeward."

"Thanks."

Swearing under his breath—mostly because he needed his breath in order to run—he turned, praying that Santa hadn't gone too far.

The cows weren't cows—they looked sort of like a cross between a bison and a sheep—but you could milk one, and if you were clever and careful—bloody careful—you could shear one. Kate and Terry had discovered them, but it was Santa who had eventually corralled them in the pen they had all so carefully built; Santa who worked at turning them into a manageable, owned herd. Or a flock, depending on who you asked. It was one of the things that the villagers had more than enough time to argue about. Funny how people always found something to argue about, and the time to argue in. For that, food, and sex. Jeremy wasn't sure whether this was a design flaw in human beings or not.

He *was* sure his pitiful ability to run was a flaw. Little Jack had come all the way from the creek without pause; his aunts and uncles could sustain that pace for half as long, and only in an emergency, only when fear was stronger than their natural desire to breathe. Jeremy didn't stop. But he prayed.

It was funny how a man who didn't believe in God could still remember, could in fact never forget, how to pray.

Santa was with the cows.

Jeremy could hear their obdurate snort-and-bleat before he could see them. He couldn't hear Santa at all, but that wasn't unusual; Santa didn't talk much, with or without cows. But the cows were essential to their survival, and

where they went, if they were away from their rough pasture, Santa went as well. He was faster than the jackals.

Not real jackals; they had more in common with wolves or wild dogs. But no one wanted to call them that, and the villagers settled on the term jackal; they were carrion creatures, the old jackals, and the village was often close enough to edge of death and starvation that the circling of the beasts *was* carrion creature behavior.

They'd lost a couple of people to the packs. Made them feel less secure about the beauty of nature, although most of them had pretty much given the romantic vision of the wilderness up to the practical, back-breaking reality of life lived in it.

"Santa!"

When he moved at all, he moved *quickly*. And quietly. He was at Jeremy's side before Jeremy could speak again—which was probably a good thing considering just how little breath he had left to speak with.

"Terry." Jeremy said, his back already bent, his hands gripping his knees. "Apple Creek. Strangers."

A big, rough staff was shoved into his hands or, rather, rapped across his knuckles until he had the sense to let go of his knees and grab it.

"Take care of the cows." Santa was gone as quickly and as silently as he'd arrived.

Jeremy used the staff as an ineffectual bat, and began to drive the herd back to their corral in the village. The beasts were big and their hides were as thick as Old Callie's; he had to put some serious muscle behind the heavy wooden staff just to make sure they could feel it. He didn't make the mistake of coming at them head-on; that had been tried once or twice, and even if the villagers were trapped in a world for which they were manifestly unprepared, they *weren't* stupid. They learned.

Still, the cows were as stubborn as proverbial donkeys—not a single villager had ever had to deal with a donkey, but they'd all heard stories—and ill-tempered in a not-too-dangerous way. Jeremy had his work cut out for him. The beasts obeyed Santa. Probably because he looked as if he'd kill them without shedding a tear over it.

They all thought that about him. Cows. Villagers. Santa wasn't an easy man to either know or like.

And too easy to depend on by far.

Jeremy swore at one of the females of the herd as she stepped on his foot, though she didn't actually put all of her weight into it. He gave her rump a heavy blow; she snorted. This was the usual interplay between creatures that had almost an order of magnitude differentiating both their weights and their intelligences.

At least it gave him something to do besides worry.

Strangers were dangerous to a village like Childhood's End. Not because they were organized and deadly—they weren't—but because they were usually desperate and deadly. Men and women still trickled through the cracks between worlds, for vastly different reasons.

Sometimes they could be incorporated into Childhood's End; a life on the edge with no way out but hard work and a lot of luck had a way of pulling people together, no matter what their previous background.

Sometimes they couldn't be.

The "couldn't be's" caused the most trouble. They'd worked hard on the village; they'd put everything—their own life's blood, their *lives*—into building it. And there wasn't much, frankly, that they wouldn't do to protect what they'd built. They hadn't had to face that truth often. But they came to understand that they—raised in a middle-class, well-pleased environment, with boundaries and rules and laws—would kill, if necessary, to protect their fragile home. It was an uncomfortable truth, as truths often were.

They'd been spared most of the killing. Most.

But before Childhood's End had been named—just before—men had come through the Toronto mirror. It had to be the Toronto mirror; they were in good shape, they couldn't have traveled any distance—not that the location of the mirror on the home world was a certain guarantee of where those who crossed it would end up in the Mirrorworld. The men had wanted to take by force what the villagers had worked so hard—even died—to build.

Jeremy hit another cow for good measure; it was getting too close to his feet.

Too much to think about, and all of his thoughts dark ones. Jeremy squinted a moment into the afternoon sunlight and then concentrated on the cows. Tried not to worry about Terry, about whether or not he'd found Santa in time, about whether or not Santa would find her in time, if time was of the essence.

By the time he got back to the village, he'd have his answer one way or the other.

It was comfortable to hate the cows. It was a distraction; he took the opportunity to enjoy it as he struggled to close the gate behind them. It was a log gate, hinged by thick rope they'd made out of reeds smashed with rocks into stringy mush; these days that rope was more valuable than money was in the old world.

It was funny, though. He could still remember his PIN for the ATM machine.

And his birthday. Although they had tried to keep calendar dates the same, the seasons didn't quite correspond to Earth's. In the end they'd been forced to add the month of Mirror to balance it all out.

They'd lost practically everything by coming across the mirror; the world itself seemed intent on expunging what little they had left from Earth—even the tiniest details: if not the fact of birth, then the rituals of it.

Santa had showed up during the month of Mirror, a year—no, two—after the first villagers had arrived. He was the tallest man in Childhood's End, and his physique was oddly perfect—the result of hard work, not hours at a gym. He was clearly well-fed. Most recent arrivals were starving. He was nothing like the usual refugees from the mirror. They'd been afraid of him; they still were.

He'd stayed a few days, nosing around a bit, asking a bunch of questions. There was an air of desperation about each and every one of those questions—and nobody wanted to make a man like that more desperate by refusing to answer.

They might not have noticed just how dangerous he was had they been living back in Toronto comfortably wrapped up in their old lives. Things were clearer here: They knew death when it stared them in the face. They had no police to call, no legal code to stand on, or lawyers to stand behind, as the case might be. They dealt with what life handed them—it was all they could do.

So the villagers, Jeremy included, answered Santa's questions as politely—and as completely—as they could without knowing which of the hundreds of queries were the relevant ones. One or two questions had to be relevant, but they didn't sift; they didn't want to disturb whatever lay in wait behind the man's neutral, but deadly, facade.

He caused them no trouble, and as the days passed, they got used to him. He liked to work while he talked, so he'd join the villagers. During the daylight hours, they all worked. During the nights they were usually too damned tired to do anything but sleep.

He slept outdoors for the most part; he'd accept the offer of a roof—shabby though those roofs were in that first couple of years—if it was raining heavily. He had equipment with him—canvas tenting with hardwood poles, a down vest, cotton nets, silk twine for snares and fishing line, bone hooks, ivory knives, candles, a bow and arrows. They all wondered how he'd managed to be so damned lucky, that he could come so well prepared.

But they wondered quietly. They didn't press him.

And one day Santa had asked Old Callie if he could make Childhood's End his home. She said yes—she was no fool. But on that day, he stopped asking questions. Stopped talking much at all, really.

She rounded up the villagers to help him put up one of the tottering shacks that passed for homes. He'd refused their help. That made him popular with Allan and Jeremy.

On the first occasion when he'd cracked a smile, they realized that he wasn't all that much older than they were.

But they only saw him smile twice.

Kate screamed when Terry came running into the village. Her cry was as good an alarm as the village had, and people responded instantly; they'd been waiting for trouble. Jeremy had managed to pen the cows without collecting anything nastier than a few bruises, and he found that he wasn't as exhausted as he'd thought. He cleared the common in under two minutes, planting his feet between the rows of green that were growing there as naturally as if he'd done it all his life—and that life depended on it.

Allan was already there, kneeling in front of Terry, his body blocking her from view.

"What happened?"

Allan didn't answer; not with words. Bad sign. Instead, he stood and stepped to the side.

Blood made Terry's face momentarily unrecognizable; it was a mask through which her eyes opened wide. Too wide. Jeremy knelt, taking Allan's place; of the two of them, he was better with startled creatures. "Terry?"

"He's going to kill her," she said, her voice high, her words a thin veneer over panic.

"Who, Terry?" Jeremy cringed as she ran the back of her hand over her eyes.

"Santa," she said. "He's going to kill them both!"

He caught her by both arms. Shook her gently. "What happened?" This close, he could see that most of the blood came from a sharp gash across her

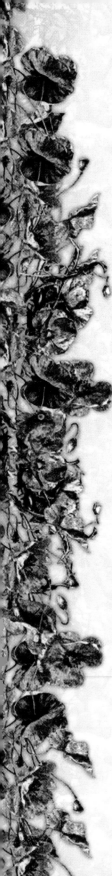

brow; it was the kind of cut that would scar, but become invisible in the inevitable creases that adults developed. It wasn't, thank God, serious.

"She pulled me out of the tree. The man with her tried to catch me, but he missed—I cut my face—"

"Who made you fall?"

"It was my fault—she wasn't angry until I kicked her in the face."

"You kicked someone in the face?"

"She was trying to grab me, to get me down from the tree, and I—I kicked her nose." She reached out suddenly, grabbed both of his hands. "He's going to kill her because she hit me. We've got to stop him!"

Allan and Jeremy locked eyes for just a moment; Allan looked away first. There were strangers, they both knew, that the village was better off without. Santa spared them from that, from having to do the killing themselves. They said that it didn't matter whose hand the blood was on—but it wasn't true; every time they were forced to kill it cost them dearly, as if the price to be paid for extinguishing life was life. And maybe these strangers were threats that had to be dealt with.

But even so, Terry would carry the weight of that guilt, and she wasn't adult, not yet. They couldn't make that choice for her at this moment, even if, in the end, something had to be done. Killing these people now would scar the girl for life.

"Get Callie," Jeremy told Kate. "Tell her we might have stranger trouble."

"She's not deaf and she's not bloody stupid," Old Callie said. She stood beside the well, leaning on a cow staff as if it were a bat and she were next up. "Neither is Terry. Terry, you think these strangers are safe?"

Terry nodded.

"But they treed you?"

"Mostly safe."

"Then don't just stand there weeping and gawking. *Let's move.*"

He was called Santa by Childhood's End because his only real interest was in the children. Not that he was overly indulgent—he wasn't—or particularly paternal; he was rather like an old testament guardian angel, with a flaming sword in one hand, and a shield in the other. It was as if he, a stranger to them all, had grasped early on the importance of the children to the psyche of the village.

He was not close to them; it was almost as if he was afraid that by touching them, he might break them somehow. But he listened to them—they all did—and he let them play their games at his feet, on them, over them. It was a rare,

rare moment when he could be convinced to join them, and the children, as if by unspoken mutual consent, hardly asked.

But if they did ask, he let his quiet dignity slip a moment. Not enough to smile, but enough to relax.

Terry was the first child who had cajoled him into her circle because she was the oldest, but the others followed, and he treated them all with that same distant affection.

Nothing bad could happen to either the cows or the kids when Santa watched over them.

If there was any truth the village could be certain of in this place where death was so prevalent, it was that.

Terry led them back the way she'd come, pausing only long enough to fret about how slowly everyone else ran. Jack kept pace with her, and Jeremy noticed that she gave up quickly on the idea of leaving the boy behind.

"Santa!"

Apple Creek, if you ignored the crashing that accompanied their hurried movements through the undergrowth, was uncomfortably silent. But silence was better than what they heard when the silence was finally broken by something that wasn't contained within the human knot they formed: a terrible bleat of pain and fear. And, weeping, a man's voice.

Terry shouted again. Her voice was a child's voice—that mixture of uncertainty and imperiousness—but her fears were already one foot across the unseen bridge that separated children from adults.

Jack joined his high voice to hers. None of the adults spoke Santa's name; it was the children's voices, after all, that had always caught his attention.

The weeping stopped. A hoarse and damaged voice called weakly for help, gurgling like a water pipe with too much air trapped in it.

God, Santa, Jeremy thought. *What the hell have you done?*

"Santa, *please*," the children called. The Magic Word.

It was like a spell of command, the word of God, it had that power for them. No one doubted that he would come.

The trees parted. Santa came out from between them, his head bowed, his fists clenched and trembling as if, Jeremy thought, he came against his will; as if a geas had been laid upon him and he had no choice but to follow.

He knelt before Terry, his hands held behind his broad back.

"You didn't—you didn't kill them, did you?" she asked.

No answer.

"Santa—you didn't—you didn't hurt them just because of *me*?" She didn't

have enough experience not to ask questions she really didn't want answers to. Maybe because she hadn't the experience to know, yet, when the answer was completely obvious.

Santa stood up then and began to walk away. Just turned his back, drew his hands out of their sight, in front of his chest, tucked his chin that way as well, chest-ward. Out of their sight. Santa's hands, Jeremy knew, must be covered in blood.

"Santa, come back!" Jack shouted.

Terry said nothing, torn a moment between the desperate need to hear his answer, even if it meant forcing the answer from him, and the certain knowledge that all she had to do was walk through those trees and she'd have it.

Torn.

And then she made her decision, and Jeremy felt something inside him snap. Break, maybe. He watched; he could not, quite, think of stopping her as she strode forward through the trees, pushing the leaves aside to get at the truth they protected.

Jack ran after Santa.

Which was good, because when it finally came, Terry's scream was quiet enough, and short enough, that he didn't have to hear it.

The truth was complicated.

In the old world—a world that wasn't, in the end, either Terry's or Jack's—the answer would have been different. There, they had hospitals, they had surgeons, they had blood—and they had antibiotics. Here? They had hot water. Wood for splints, thick cloth to bind with. Alcohol, of sorts, but nothing good, and not enough of it.

They might have saved her, there.

God—the woman. Her face. Her arms—the welts across her chest, arms, legs…Santa had been in a fight or two in his time; they all had. But Santa's fights had been with strangers; he had never lifted his hand to a villager. They knew, therefore, that he was capable of violence, but the violence was remote. It was in their defense. Violence of defense—self-defense—didn't count somehow. But *this* was different.

Why? Because they hadn't seen the others? Or because Terry stood like a rigid statue, a slender thing of stone and fear and guilt, all of which robbed Jeremy of the remove necessary to look on violence as an act of survival—as an action that was anything other than what it was: This. Shattering.

The man—husband, they thought—that had been the woman's companion clearly had a broken arm, a broken shoulder. He had tried to come to her defense, and he had been shrugged off with enough force to carry him fifteen

feet, maybe more—none of it cleared. He'd been stupid enough to get up again, to keep coming; there were purple-red marks in his throat that lined up exactly with Santa's grip. It was a miracle that the man's windpipe hadn't been crushed by the pressure; they'd seen Santa do that to a jackal before.

Old Callie and Helen knelt beside the woman, obscuring her face.

Jeremy reached out to touch Terry's shoulder; she shrugged his hand off. Would not meet his eyes, or anyone else's. He thought, *You're only ten, Terry. Ten.* But ten in a world like this might be a third of her life. Half. All.

She stood.

Throughout it all, the man, in a state of terror, of shock, kept asking the same question over and over. *Why?*

They had no answer to give him.

They carried her out of the forest. A stretcher, made of the rough woolen blankets that had come, with such painful effort, from the coats of cows, was brought, and they very gingerly lifted the woman from the forest floor. It wouldn't have been the right thing to do in the old world; in the old world, someone qualified to move a person with broken bones would have been called. They made do.

Helen was—had been—a nurse. Old Callie had been—well, no one really knew what she'd been. She didn't say. They didn't ask. They had learned, *very* quickly, that she was raised in a generation where it was more polite to ask a woman about the intimate details of her sex life than her age. Still, she had a good hand for nursing, and when Helen made her decisions, she looked to Callie for approval.

There were three nurses in Childhood's End because the mirror had opened up close to a stretch of hospitals. Opened up close to the University of Toronto, as it bisected University Avenue, passing *through* the large, mirrored office building that lay at its beginning. They picked up a few entrepreneurs that day, a lot of Bay Street officionados who had made their living pushing both paper and virtual money from one end of a computer to the other. They also had three doctors, all surgeons, who had been pretty damned close to the mirror the day the bugs had come through. A great many people fled mirrorward to escape— not because that was intelligent, but because the bugs were going in the other direction, and the people wanted to be at their backs, not near their mandibles.

There had been, of course, a general quarantine of the Mirror area itself. But it was hard to quarantine a city like Toronto; the downtown core was exactly that: the center of the city. Its heart. There were high-rise condominiums and very old row houses tucked into side-streets that were all a stone's throw from

the mirror's surface. Hell, there were buildings that the mirror passed *through*. People had to get home, and even if they were told to stay there, they were still just too damned close.

"Doctor Stephens is waiting," Allan said, interrupting Jeremy's internal history. He bent at the knees. Put his hands round both poles and gripped them firmly.

Jeremy picked up the other side, sliding hands round the poles. They counted to three and then rose slowly, letting their knees take the stress of the lift. Helen and Doctor Stephens had made it perfectly clear that it was vital to lift a person with broken bones as smoothly as possible, and with as little jarring.

Which was a pain when speed was also of the essence.

Jeremy very much doubted that speed was of the essence here. One way or the other it was just a matter of time.

The stranger wouldn't say what he'd done to get delivered to this side of the mirror. What he would say, what was absolutely clear, was that the mirror, over the years, had become a cheap alternative to a messy murder. The mirrors had slowly destroyed the city core, and because of that, because of the abandonment of the buildings and land that had once been so defining to Toronto, they had become too accessible to the city's criminal element. Toss the victim through, and the crook didn't have to pay for the bullet or dispose of the corpse.

Confronted with a gun—which seemed as mythic to him now as a sword did—Jeremy would have probably taken his chances with the mirror, too.

But it would have been a cleaner death, that gun.

It was getting darker by the time they reached home; they had to walk carefully, choose every step, match every up and down as much as they could. It was tiring, and they stopped twice to change positions. Jeremy thought his knees wouldn't take it; they struggled their way into Childhood's End.

Torches were burning. The doctors were up, and pacing, when they at last reached the Stephens' house. Helen ran ahead to say lord only knew what to Doctor Stephens; their heads were bent together as if they were discussing something secret, something important, in front of their children.

And they were, in a sense; Terry was there, silent, a witness.

The woman's husband was led away by Doctor Perth. The man's sharp cry of pain as his arm was splinted and tied flat to his chest could be heard clear across the village.

Old Callie slipped away, and Jeremy saw her leave.

Doctor Stephens and Helen were dripping sweat, squinting into the dying light as they worked. The woman had bones broken, yes, and teeth. Helen seemed happy that the jaw was only broken in two places and not shattered, which was what she'd expected. Jeremy could hear Helen's dispassionate catalogue of the woman's injuries.

"Terry?" he said, but she wouldn't leave.

And he, alas, couldn't stay. He followed Old Callie out, into a sky where the other planets were apparent, and the stars would become more so as the night wore on.

Nights like this, with the stars so piercingly clear—and so utterly familiar now, so many years later, that he had almost lost a sense of what the night sky over Toronto looked like—Jeremy could take a breath of air that was free of carcinogens, of nicotine, of strange perfumes and the haze that came with living in a city. He could take that breath, hold it, let it out slowly, and see the sky.

There was so little that made the wilderness beautiful that he had to make

himself stop and appreciate it when it struck him that way: wild and beautiful. Tomorrow it would be the faceless enemy again, the thing that worked against them, like weather, like too hot a summer, too wet a spring, too cold—God-if-he-existed protect them from this—too cold a winter.

"Where do you think you're going?" Callie said sharply.

"Following you," was Jeremy's mild reply. He fell into step with her, as if they were both old soldiers.

"Where's Jack?"

"Little Jack?" Jeremy shrugged. "He followed Santa."

No question at all that he'd be safe with Santa, even after what they'd seen. To his surprise, Callie said, "Good. Means he won't be able to run away."

"Jack?"

"Idiot."

They walked into the darkness. The light from the borealis effect was bright enough that they needed no torches, and in Jeremy's opinion that wasn't going to change; the sky was too damned clear.

"I'd send you home," Callie said abruptly. "But I might need you. You talk when I tell I you to talk, you shut up until then. Clear?"

It took all of his effort to swallow to swallow at least three sarcastic replies. He nodded instead. She was, after all, carrying the heavy wooden staff that they used to nudge cows with; against people it would be rather more effective.

She could probably hear the replies he had to bite his tongue not to make; she squinted at him, rather than glaring. Her eyes were terrible, and they'd not the means to grind glass; hell, they barely had the means to make it at this point. That was one of the things that Jackson had been refining when he died.

One day, Jeremy thought, she'd see again, clearly. But nearsighted and hobbled by that lack of vision as she was, Callie was formidable. She didn't have half her teeth either; she'd been the first to have them pulled.

I know my teeth, goddammit, she'd said, to a visibly green Doctor Stephens. *And I don't care if you aren't a dentist. You pull 'em before they kill me.* And he had. No one offered much resistance to Old Callie, even if it meant they had to roll up their sleeves and do the dirty work.

"Should have had this out years ago," Callie said, the anger in the words clearly aimed at herself.

"Had what out?"

"Did I tell you to speak?"

He sighed.

"Good. If you were Allan, I'd send you packing. That boy doesn't know when to shut up."

He rolled his eyes; in the night, with her vision, that was safe. Of course, she wasn't stupid, so she thumped him anyway.

They hadn't walked that far—maybe halfway to Santa's place—when they found Jack. Or rather, Jack found them. You wouldn't think hair that burr-tangled could shine in the starlight, but it did. So did the tear tracks on his cheeks.

"Jack?" Jeremy called him, quietly, casting a sideways glance at Old Callie. Old Callie wasn't as good with children as she could be; she said she was so old she couldn't remember how to sound like anything other than who she was anymore.

She didn't thump him.

Jack came running to Jeremy immediately. "You've got to stop him!"

"Stop him?"

Old Callie swore.

It was village doctrine that there was to be no swearing of any sort around the children. God knows why; in this place, swearing was a useful skill. But they restrained themselves. And when they didn't, it meant something.

"Stop him from doing what, Jack?" Jeremy asked.

"Leaving!"

"What?"

"He's going to pack up his things. He don't have much. He's leaving."

Callie swore some more, and loudly, for good measure. "Should've had this out *years* ago." She thrust the cow-staff into Jeremy's hands. "Go after him. Stop him."

"But—"

Her voice was as intense as the light in the darkness. "You don't understand what he is, Jeremy. And even if you did, it wouldn't matter. How do you think we've made it this far? Who brought us the cows? Who drove out the jackals? Who set up the trapping lines for fur so that we never had to go through a winter like that first one again? I don't care what he was. I don't care what he is. This village depends on him." She gave the wooden staff a shove; it thudded gently against his chest. "I'm not going to get there before he leaves. You will. Don't screw up."

"Callie, just what the hell is he?"

"Human being, same as the rest of us." Her gaze perched a moment on the top of Jack's head. "Jack, go to your mother."

"But—"

"Now."

"I have five minutes. You get the short story. You tell anyone else and I'll kill you."

The ritual disclaimer for Callie. No one had died yet. Jeremy nodded.

"He came here looking for something. Found it when he found those kids. But when he asked me if he could stay, he was worried about what he was, and what he'd do." Callie paused. "Back home, after that first day, things flew *out* of the mirrors. Giant bugs. Bigger than about four people put together. People died. A lot of them. Now, this'll really shock you. The U.N. got together and did something useful."

"You're right. I don't believe you."

She ignored him. "They recruited a bunch of people—and quick—and they put them through tests. Physical tests. Mental tests. They chose some sixty or so. And they rebuilt 'em from the inside out."

"*What?*"

"They rebuilt 'em. See, some people made it back to the other side—so they knew that metal, plastics, anything inorganic—disappeared in the crossing. So they couldn't give their regular soldiers weapons and send 'em across; they had to make their weapons. Sixty men and women. They peeled off their skins, practically; turned their minds inside out; made them soldier Bug-killers from hell. Some of 'em went off the deep end. Hell, they probably all did, and it'll be years before the cracks show. Just like with Santa. He told me that," she added, her voice softening. "They came through the mirrors to do what they were made for—and there was nothing to fight. Just us."

"You said there were sixty like him?"

"No. Sixty to start. I don't remember how many made it." She turned away. "He told me because he was afraid that he wasn't human enough to live with us; that he'd been made to kill; that he'd volunteered for something different than what he got, and he'd lost everything important in the process.

"I told him that we'd worry about it when it happened." Jeremy thought, suddenly, that he could see tears on her cheeks. "So it's happened," she said gruffly. "You go get him, boy. Bring him back."

He was called Santa in Childhood's End because of the children.

Because he thought—no one really understood why, not after that first year, when the winter nearly killed them all—that Christmas was important. Given that roughly a third of their number were Jewish, and that the Anglican affiliation of the majority was a cultural designation and not a matter that necessitated great faith, his insistence was met with a certain nervous resignation. It was the first time that he had asked for anything.

He went out and found a tree. Took a stone axe to cut it down with. They'd known he was strong of course, but they were still damned surprised to see him dragging a spruce-like tree across the snow's surface. Not that there was much snow; had there been, had it been a cold enough climate for that, they would never have made it another year.

He set up the tree, and the children watched in fascination. But only one of them remembered why. Some dim memory. Something that was years old. Terry had walked over the tree, touching its branches as they shook and jiggled while people tried to stand it up in the dirt and rock pit that, in the summer, was the heart of their communal fire. In the winter, it was just too much out in the open.

"Santa," she said, looking up at the man who had brought the tree in. He smiled at her. The first time. And then, her expression crumbled, "Mommy and Daddy." She didn't cry. Susan picked her up before she could even really begin to look upset. But her voice was quiet. Very quiet.

"Remember what I told you, Terry? Mommy and Daddy are dead."

"I know," she replied. "But I miss them very much." She paused. "Will we have a star on the top of the tree? Will there be presents?"

Susan smiled a little. "We'll make do."

They were all surprised; Susan said afterward that Terry probably had barely been speaking when she'd last celebrated Christmas. And Santa—well, he called himself Santa after that. He found some things for her—wooden things, a roughly carved cow, a funny little wagon—things that were clearly the product of his own labor.

He found the tree every year. Brought it in. Brought presents that became more elaborate as he understood his tools and his materials better.

Jeremy thought, with a pang, that they would miss Christmas if Santa were gone, because it came with him, a force of his nature, and it would probably leave with him as well. A smarter person would have been worried about the cows. Jackals. Strangers. About the winter hunting. Hard to find a balance between the things that one needed to survive, and the things that one needed so that survival seemed like a worthwhile goal.

Jeremy ran.

It occurred to him later that if Santa hadn't wanted to be caught, he wouldn't have been caught. He had better night vision than anyone, and he could run through a forest in the dark without snapping a branch. Not without making noise, though—Jeremy didn't hear much in the way of noise.

Santa's shack was empty; that much he'd expected. What he hadn't quite expected was that so little would be taken from it. There were things that were piled in the corner by the door, and one of them made Jeremy stop dead. He held his breath as he reached out to touch it, needing tactile confirmation in the shadows: It was a book.

Nothing made him cry, not even being here. This book was probably the thing that had come closest since they named the village. He couldn't make out what the words on the cover were. Didn't know what the book was about. It almost didn't matter. Jeremy's desire to read words—almost any words—was visceral enough that he made it half-way out of the dwelling clutching the book as if it were a terrible secret.

He shook himself. Looked around. Blankets were here. The rough knife

they'd made when they'd found the bog iron fifteen miles from the village. Everything but some clothing, some fur. He wasn't certain, but he thought that the cured meat had been left intact as well.

But if Santa wanted to leave the village without interference, he had to go west.

Jeremy closed the door, and began to follow in what he hoped were Santa's footsteps. Damned fool thing to do, at this time of night; he only meant to go as far as the outer edge of the cleared land and return. But he got as far as the graveyard instead, which was closer.

And there, he saw Santa, kneeling in the tall grass and the weeds that were another continuous battle for anyone who thought a graveyard should have well-tended dignity.

"Go away."

Jeremy stopped moving. The breeze in the trees and the blades of grass and weed-leaf was more dynamic than he. "Old Callie sent me."

Santa said nothing.

"She wanted to come herself, but she thought you'd be moving too quickly."

Santa didn't even turn. But he answered. "I had my good-byes to say. And I want to say them in peace. *Go away.*"

Jeremy heard it then: the wild anger that struggled beneath the surface of all of Santa's words and actions. It had broken through, in the forest by Apple Creek. Jeremy was very much concerned that it would break through again in the graveyard of Childhood's End. He almost left.

But as he made fists of his hands, he felt the leather-bound cover of a book stop them in mid-curl. Santa's book. "I—you left something."

"I left a lot of things."

There was a little light. Jeremy held the book up, and he could read what was written there, because the embossed letters shone—and because he suddenly knew which book it was. He'd once owned it.

Santa rose. "You want it? Take it." Bitter words. "It was for her, anyway. I couldn't stand it, but it was her favorite book—elves, dwarves, and all. *The Lord of the Rings.*" More words, Jeremy thought, said at one time than Santa'd ever said to the rest of the village. "I knew. I knew that we'd have to pack carefully. I couldn't bring her anything else that was hers, that I'd given her. Not the rings. Not the necklaces." Jeremy didn't cry. And Santa didn't. It wasn't the kind of release they'd ever allow themselves.

"Terry didn't even recognize me. I knew they'd changed me. My skin and part of my muscle structure—they had to rebuild it. I don't understand why. But I knew I could convince Karen who I was, if I could find her. I knew that. She knew *me.*" He sat down again, on the grassy ground before the graves, and

Jeremy saw that he did, indeed, sit before the rough wooden cross that had been made for Karen. Terry's mother.

"You don't know," he said. "You don't know what it was like. No one told me, you know? I was watching the goddamn television and I saw it. In replay, over and over—I can *still* see it whenever I close my eyes. Terry ran toward the mirror; Karen shouted—screamed—and Terry just disappeared. What else could Karen do? She had to follow. She left the stroller behind, she just ran—"

Jeremy sat down on the ground, though not beside Santa, not exactly.

"I didn't know if they'd been eaten alive but I thought—I thought I would know, I would know here, if she'd been taken away from me." He turned then, and spit. "I was such a stupid—it never occurred to me that Terry would survive and Karen—" Silence was his punctuation.

Jeremy was glad that it was dark, now.

"Even if she didn't recognize me, I'd gone through everything to find them. Karen wasn't here. Terry was. I thought I could protect her." He lifted his hands. "I made it my life, you know? To protect her." Lowered them again.

Really, really glad that it was dark.

Did you never think of telling her the truth? But he didn't ask. There wasn't much he could say.

"I'm not a monster," Santa said, with no conviction. "She hit my daughter—that woman—after everything I'd done. They pulled her out of the tree—she fell—she hit my daughter—" Silence again. Santa rose. "And I can't tell her now, can I? I think I did more damage to Terry today than anyone's ever done in her life.

"The worst part is, I don't know that I wouldn't do it again—I just snapped, and when I was finished…. I don't want to leave." He picked up the leather backpack that he'd come with years ago. "But I can't face Terry. I can't tell her the truth." Men like Santa didn't cry. But the light glinted silver on his cheeks, a thin trail on either side of his face. "Nobody wants a monster for a father."

"Why don't you let her decide that?"

Old Callie's voice. They both turned. And in the light of Mirrorworld's borealis, they could see that Terry stood beside her.

Santa bolted.

Terry hesitated just a minute, and then she ran after him, into the darkness, crying out his name. "*Santa! Santa! DADDY!*"

"Callie," Jeremy said quietly. "You're a bitch."

"Yep. A smart one. Give a half-blind old woman an arm before she crashes into something meaner than she is."

"How did you know?"

"Didn't. I just figured that she'd have to have it out with him one way or
the other, for her own sake. I didn't know how it would turn out. I guess we
were lucky."

They listened a moment, as the sounds of running stopped. Jeremy knew
they'd have to. Santa could run full pace through a dark forest, but he knew that
Terry couldn't. He wouldn't risk losing her in the forest at night. Not when the
jackals were out.

"You think he'll be okay?"

"I don't know," she said. "But even Superman needed his friends. No happy
endings here, just tolerable ones. Compromised ones."

"Childhood's End."

"Whatever."

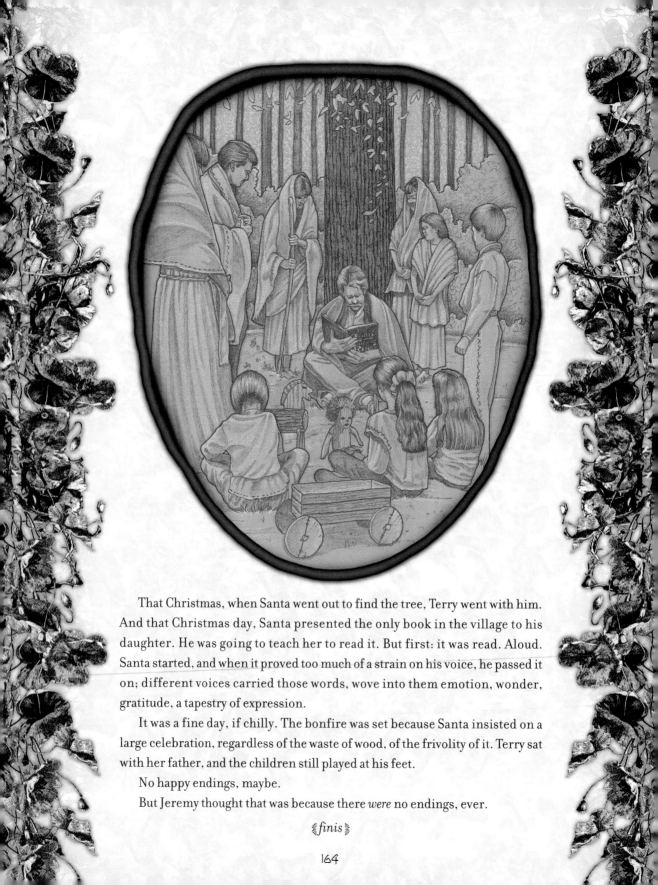

That Christmas, when Santa went out to find the tree, Terry went with him. And that Christmas day, Santa presented the only book in the village to his daughter. He was going to teach her to read it. But first: it was read. Aloud. Santa started, and when it proved too much of a strain on his voice, he passed it on; different voices carried those words, wove into them emotion, wonder, gratitude, a tapestry of expression.

It was a fine day, if chilly. The bonfire was set because Santa insisted on a large celebration, regardless of the waste of wood, of the frivolity of it. Terry sat with her father, and the children still played at his feet.

No happy endings, maybe.

But Jeremy thought that was because there *were* no endings, ever.

finis

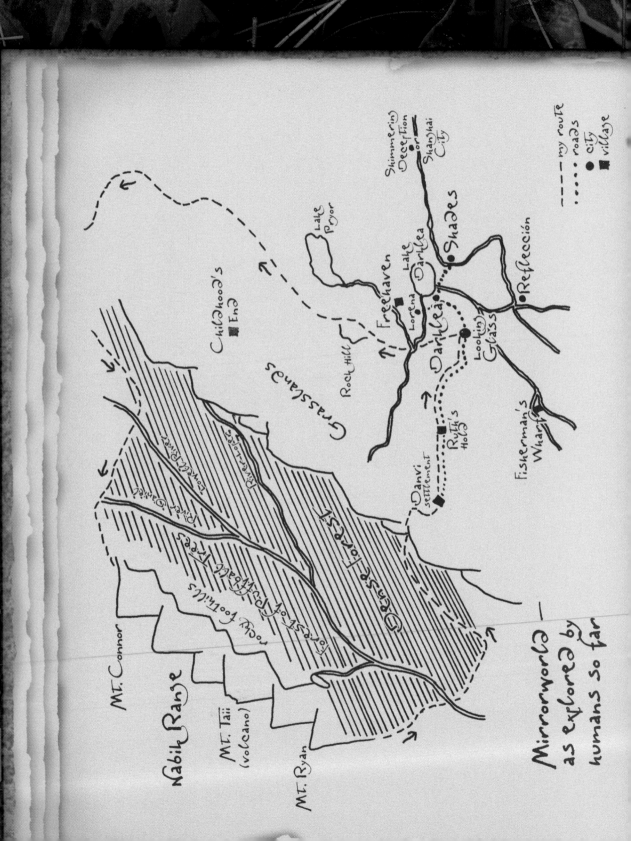

Nabik Range

Mt. Connor

Mt. Taii (volcano)

Mt. Ryan

Rocky Foothills

Forest-to-Foothills Transition Trees

River Darñea

River-of-Tears

Dense Forest

Danvi Settlement

Ruth's Hold

Fisherman's Wharf

Childhood's End

Grasslands

Rock Hill

Lake Pryor

Freehaven

Lorena

Lake Darñea

Darñea

Looking Glass

Shades

Reflección

Shimmering Deception or

Shanghai City

Mirrorworld —
as explored by
humans so far

---- my route
···· roads
● city
▪ village

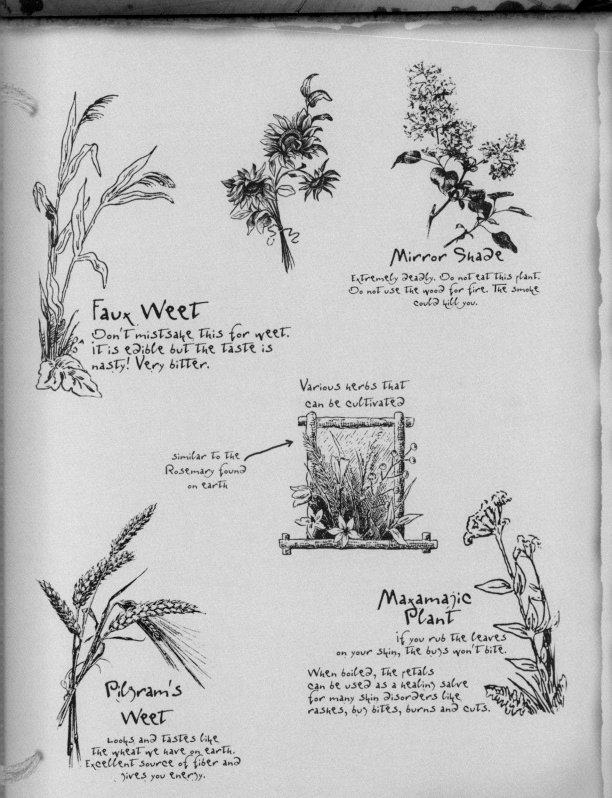

Mirror Shade

Extremely deadly. Do not eat this plant. Do not use the wood for fire. The smoke could kill you.

Faux Weet

Don't mistsake this for weet. It is edible but the taste is nasty! Very bitter.

Various herbs that can be cultivated

similar to the Rosemary found on earth

Maxamajic Plant

If you rub the leaves on your skin, the bugs won't bite.

When boiled, the petals can be used as a healing salve for many skin disorders like rashes, bug bites, burns and cuts.

Pilgram's Weet

Looks and tastes like the wheat we have on earth. Excellent source of fiber and gives you energy.

My old friend Rain is one of the toughest women I've ever met. She came across the mirror with me and found her calling in the city of Looking Glass working for the good of the city and its people.

75th day after entry into Mirrorworld...

Today i begin my exploration of this world in earnest. i have been supplied with what meager provisions the villagers of Lorena were able to provide. My hope is to catalogue some of the many different types of flora and fauna in this strange new world.

79th day...

After striking north for several days, i followed a river back to a large lake. Water sources seem potable and, more important, plentiful. What appears to be rolling grasslands stretch out as far as the eye can see. Little in the way of wildlife on the open plains. Perhaps i'll find examples elsewhere.

Have started toxicity tests on various plants (see sketches). Will look for others during my travels. if possible will collect samples to dry and press.

52nd day...

Came across one of the more unusual specimens of plant life today. In a small valley, i passed through several acres of what resembled our sunflowers back on Earth. They were about eight feet tall, with fern-like leaves on their stalks and a round black pistil surrounded by red, blue, and purple petals. The odd thing about these plants is that as soon as i entered the field, their heads all turned to face me, and followed my progress. i was careful not to step on any of them, unsure as to whether they had any defenses. nevertheless, it was a bit unnerving being watched by several dozen plants every step i took. No samples collected.

58th day...

It looks like i'll be coming to a vast forest in the next week or so. i can see the line of trees where it begins, but trying to estimate distance here is next to impossible.

Found another unusual plant today, one that seems a little more dangerous. It has a stem like a rose, with very sharp thorns. It has bright red blossoms, apparently to attract animal life, of which several skeletons remained underneath. i could not see exactly how the plants subdued the animals, and didn't want to approach to find out. Several bird carcasses were there, as well as some sort of primate. Could not examine remains any closer.

63rd day...

Supplies from village running low. i'll have to forage soon. Fortunately, i'm at the edge of the forest, and judging by the calls and signs, animal life is plentiful here.

Later, same day...

Animal life is indeed plentiful. My evening meal is the first meat i've had in weeks. It was an animal about the size of a faun with six legs and light green fur. If i hadn't been looking directly at it when it moved, i never would have seen it. The meat is tender yet gamey, but edible. Right now, i'm not complaining. Will lay up here a few days to skin and smoke the carcass. Will explore the forest further when my journey resumes...

Maxwell Blue - an old buddy, smartest guy i ever met... got a head full of trivia and a heart of gold. The brother i never had...

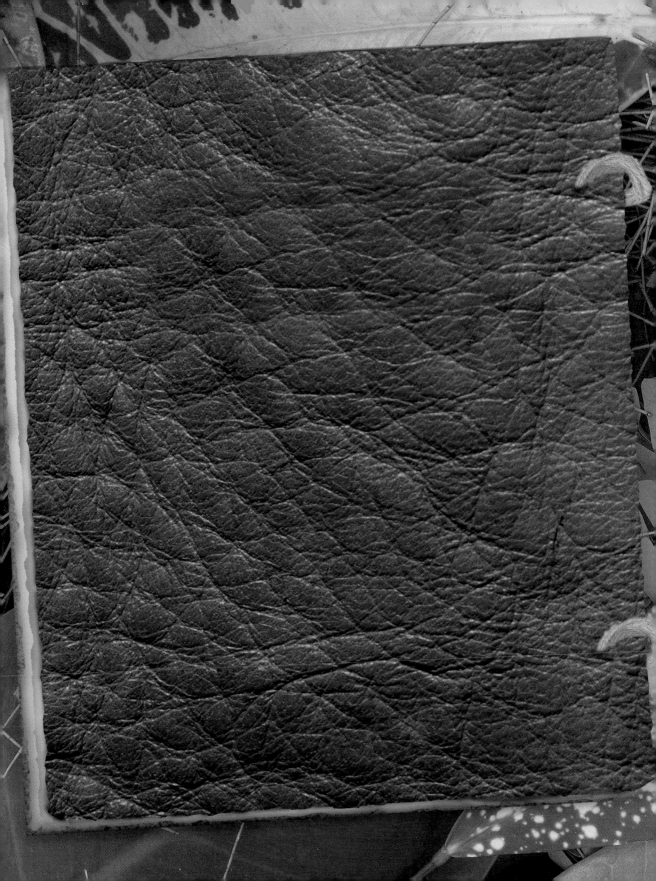